MY HOT BOSS

BETTY SHREFFLER

My Hot Boss

Copyright © 2017 by Betty Shreffler

Editor: Sandy Ebel, Personal Touch Editing

CHAPTER 1

EMMA

*E*VER HAVE ONE OF THOSE moments in your life where you think—*This. Is. Not. My. Finest. Moment?* Ever since meeting Grayson Cole, that very phrase has gone through my head far too many times. It started with the very first time I met him. My best friend Megan coaxed me, and by coaxed, I mean dragged me off my couch, threw clothes at me and demanded I come out with her or our friendship would irrevocably end. Yep, that's her. My Megan. A spunktastic, larger than life, bestie with short, jet black hair and large, brown, doe eyes. Her bold personality either terrifies you or makes you want to cuddle her. There's no in between.

Three weeks prior, my ex broke up with me. Stupid me never saw it coming. Everything in my mind was fucking fantastic, but then the terrible words dripped from his mouth. "I need some space." Those words led to him moving out of our apartment the next day while I worked my ass off, unknowing, that the last two years of my life spent building a future with him was now dust in the wind.

Walking into my apartment that afternoon was gut-wrenching. Several calls to his phone led to texts responses of, "We've grown apart." "I love you, but I need to work on me." "I've started seeing someone else." Shit, that went south fast.

Squeezing my phone in my hand as if I could crush it with pure anger, I slumped against the wall and bawled my eyes out. You know the kind of crying where snot puddles on your upper lip and you can only partially breathe through one nostril. That night I buried my feelings in a whole tub of cookies and cream and then lost all feelings at the bottom of a wine bottle followed by lighting every photo of Derrick and me on fire in my kitchen sink, which may have set off the fire alarm. Ok, that might have been my first—*This is not my finest moment.*

That all leads to Megan demanding I get beautiful, liquored up, and conquer the battlefield of love again.

DRESSED IN HEELS THAT SAY—yes, I like to fuck with nothing but these on—completes my pretty, blue, dress and long, loose waves of my chestnut hair.

Inside the bar, *Sin*, is a decor of black and white with bits of royal blue circles and swirls along the wall. If I stand in the wrong spot, between my dress and the flashing lights, my torso disappears and my head, arms, and legs glow. Not at all conducive to trying to get noticed by the opposite sex.

The bar is my refuge. Megan and I practically race there for different reasons, of course. I need the courage and to forget my lingering sorrow, while she wants to get her dancing legs ready. I finish off my Mojito as she points at potential candidates for me.

"Oh Em, what about that one?" She tilts her glass in the direction of a decent looking guy with a gray suit and perfectly cut hair talking with two of his friends.

A grimace sneaks onto my face.

Megan rolls her eyes below her long, dark lashes. "And what's wrong with that guy?"

Truth. He isn't Derrick.

"Girl, I'm telling you, the best way to start getting over Derrick is to find someone that makes you forget all about him."

"Stay out of my head."

"You need to stay out of your own head. Here, try this."

Handing me her drink, she winks and shoves it closer when I look at her questioningly.

"Oh, go on. You'll like it."

With a tilt of my head, I give in and sip the fruity alcoholic drink. Megan's hand pushes at the bottom of the glass and holds it against my lips until I finish every drop. She giggles when I remove the empty glass.

"You'll thank me later."

With the liquor warming my body, I lean against the bar and smile. "Better."

Reaching up, she slips her hand in my bent arm. "Even if you don't meet someone, it's a night off from thinking about Derrick the asshole. Now, let's go dance, pretty Princess. Maybe Prince Charming is here waiting for you to dance in front of his eyes."

It doesn't take much for the liquor to take effect, and before long, I'm losing myself to the rhythm of the music, swaying my hips and moving my arms in the air. For a time, I've forgotten all about my misery in the love department. When the song changes, I throw my thumb over my shoulder. "I'm heading to the bathroom."

Megan nods and moves toward the bar. "I'll get us more drinks."

In my haste to reach the toilet, I turn the corner and smack right into a tall man wearing a light yellow dress shirt with rolled up sleeves and charcoal gray slacks. A tattoo peeks out beneath his right sleeve and on his wrist is a shiny silver watch, giving him a professional look. As my gaze raises to his face, I have to remind myself to breathe. His brown, styled hair is spiked up every which way and a trimmed beard covers the bottom half of his beautiful face. The eyes looking back at me, though, are what makes my body pop and sizzle and my vagina scream, *him, he's the one!* Those ice blue-green eyes indicate that there's intelligence with a spark of mystery behind them. I long to know more about the mysterious bit.

"Hey Princess, you okay?" A smooth, deep baritone fills my ears, followed by Mr. Gorgeous waving his hand in my face.

A giggle escapes me. "That's what my best friend calls me."

"There she is."

I step back, realizing I'm still within his strong arms and inches from his kissable face.

"Sorry about that. I'm Emma Williams." Reaching my hand out, I await him to take it.

The corner of his mouth raises into the sexiest, humored smile I've ever seen. My vagina heats up and my heartbeat races like I've just run a marathon. That smile, those lips, the way his eyes crinkle and spark, are too hot for my lacy panties. What's left of them anyway. I'm pretty sure they melted the moment my eyes had the pleasure of meeting his handsome face.

Mr. Gorgeous takes my hand, turns it, then raises, and kisses it. The touch of his warm lips against my skin sends a flutter of arousal shooting right through me. "Nice to meet you, Emma."

Another girlish giggle slips out, embarrassing me further. "You just kissed my hand."

A brow raises as if he is challenging me to say I didn't like it. "I did. It felt right."

"You're too damn cute."

"So are you. You want to have a drink with me when you come back out?"

"Yes." The word races out of my mouth and my cheeks flush. *Too quick, Em.*

His delicious smile returns and I let out a breath. When he releases my hand, I put it back to my side, surprised at how comfortable it felt with him.

"I'll see you at the bar. What do you like to drink?"

"A blackberry Mojito."

"Nice choice." He winks, then walks away, heading to the bar.

The moment he's gone the warmth of his presence is sucked out of the air. The temperature feels cooler and my body is eager to return to him. Rushing to the bathroom, I pull my phone out of my purse and immediately text Megan. I have no shame, I pee and text.

Met hottie on way to bathroom. He is buying me a drink. Yellow shirt, gray slacks, to die for looks. Mine. All mine. ;)

When I reach the sink, my phone dings.

I see him. He's smokin'. Get it, girl. ;)

Returning to the bar has my heart pitter-pattering with excitement. I catch his attention and his incredible smile lights up his face. As I settle onto the stool next to him, he slides my drink toward me, then turns his stool to face me.

Taking the drink in my hand, I sip the refreshing liquid and smile. "Thank you—"

"Grayson Cole," he finishes.

My brows raise an inch. "Love your name. Grayson Cole. Sounds so sexy."

"Well, Princess, I do like the sound of it coming from your lips."

Warmth spreads through me and I giggle. "I like that you call me Princess."

"Good, I like it too. So, *Princess*, tell me all about you."

Swirling the tiny, red straw in my drink, I think about what to share. "How much do you want to know?"

Raising his glass to his lips, he takes a drink of what looks like whiskey or scotch, then sets his eyes on me. "Everything."

"I'm a book agent. I live around here. I don't have any pets. Would love a puppy, but I'm not home enough to care for it. I like having a drink with dinner. I eat out often. I'm not a great cook. Ok, maybe I'm a pretty good cook, but I like food better when I don't have to cook it. My guilty pleasure is chocolate, bubble baths, and erotic novels. I don't have any siblings. I love the color peach and my best friend is Megan and she's somewhere in this club."

Tapping his finger on his glass, he smiles and his square jaw flexes. My nipples harden against my dress and for the first time his eyes lower to my chest and then return to my eyes. "Erotic novels, huh?"

I laugh and bring my Mojito to my lips. "Is that all you got from that, Grayson?"

Leaning forward, he draws my body to his. Raising his hand, he swipes a loose hair and places it behind my ear. The smell of his cologne assaults my senses and I close my eyes breathing in his rich, incredible scent. My lip slides between my teeth and I open my eyes to his gaze steady on me.

"I heard every bit and, Emma Williams, I'm completely intrigued. Would you like to dance with me?"

"Yes," the word slips out of my mouth dripping with sexual desire.

Taking my hand, he leads me onto the dance floor and I slide into his arms as he wraps them around my waist, putting his chest to my back. Not only is Grayson sexy as fuck, he has moves. Moves that make my body ignite, creating sparks of arousal detonating at my core. His breath is hot on my ear as he whispers, "You smell incredible and feel even better."

A bulge is tight against my ass and I push back against him. Too many drinks and my desire has me thinking about where I'd like that bulge to end up. With those wicked thoughts flashing through my mind, he turns me to face him, and his lips claim mine. His tongue diving in and out between my lips has me so turned on I want to climb him, here, now, in front of all the people in the club. Sensing my need, he leads me off the dance floor, pins me to the nearest wall and continues his mouth fucking.

Pulling away, he takes a breath. "Emma, this is incredibly pretentious of me, but I want to take you home with me. I think you want it too."

Biting my lip, I debate; be shameless and give into my desires or slow this train before it's speeding too fast for me. Fuck it. I deserve to have an incredibly hot man make love to me, one who wants me as much as I want him. "Let's go."

Grayson takes my hand, pulling me through the crowd. Anticipation builds in my gut as we near the exit. I'm dizzy with lust and my body is warm with intense desire. Stepping out the doors, the summer heat hits me like a tidal wave. Nausea churns in my stomach. *No, no, please no, don't be sick.* My hand goes to my mouth and I turn away from Grayson. I attempt to make a mad dash back inside and I curl over. Won't be making it anywhere. I throw up into the grassy area by the doors, horrified by what just happened. I'm quickly made aware of Grayson's presence by the sound of his voice asking me if I'm okay. I open my eyes and see black shoes covered in little bits of spatter. Here you go. This is where it happens.

This. Is. Not. My. Finest. Moment.

"Oh my God. I'm so sorry," I squeak out, more embarrassed than I've ever felt in my life.

Grayson places his hand on my back and rubs gently. "Don't worry about it. They're just shoes."

I can't even look at him. Standing up straight, I wipe my mouth and then as gracefully as possible, I turn to face him. His expression is empathetic, not at all horrified like I am. Any recovery from this is impossible.

"I think I need to find Megan and call it a night."

"I understand. Let me see your phone."

Pulling it out of my purse, I hand it to him. He plugs his number in and hands it back to me. "Call me soon."

Grayson walks me back inside and when I see Megan, I point to her. "There she is. I'm gonna let her know I'm heading home. Thanks for a great night."

With a kiss to my cheek, he smiles, then leaves the club.

I rush to Megan sitting at the bar, talking to a good-looking redhead—her favorite type—and bury my face into her shoulder. She pats my cheek. "What's wrong?"

"I'm gonna head home."

"Why? What happened?"

Nodding to her male friend, I give a friendly smile, then turn to face her. "I'll explain later. Have a good rest of your night. We'll talk tomorrow."

Her bottom lip juts out. "Ok, babe. You sure?"

I nod. "Yeah, for sure. Thanks for coaxing me out." Waving, I head outside.

Once out the door, I avoid the disaster area that coils my stomach just thinking about it and pull out my phone to call a cab. Arrangements are made and as I hang up a larger man bumps into me when he opens the club door for the woman accompanying him. My body jolts forward and my phone goes flying through the air and smashes on the ground.

"Shit!"

The man doesn't even apologize. Just disappears inside without a word. Disgruntled, I quickly pick up my phone. Turning it over reveals a shattered screen. I try to turn it on and nothing. Tears prickle my eyes. With a heavy breath, I shove my phone back into my purse and fight back the returning nausea as I wait for the cab.

CHAPTER 2

EMMA

A MONTH LATER, I'M SITTING at my office desk, nibbling on my red pen as I read through a super hot sex scene from a book submission called, *She Likes It Hot*. Well, yes, this girl does. My legs are tight together; I'm getting all hot and bothered reading this scene and totally wishing I was home, alone, with my vibrator.

This past month I've daydreamed one too many times about Grayson Cole. Because life likes to torture me, I was never able to call him. I had to replace my phone and any new contacts that had been added since my last backup were gone. I tried to Facebook stalk Grayson with no success. Who doesn't have a Facebook nowadays? I thought it was mandatory for anyone under thirty-five.

So now, because of him, and my unquenched desires, I've been reading every erotic book submission in my email this past month. This one is particularly naughty and I'm loving it, but not my current reading location.

I rub my thighs together as another wave of arousal moves through my body. Fuck, this book is good. Definitely sending this author kudos and a contract.

A tap on my door jolts my body, and I drop my pen. I clear my throat and with flushed cheeks, I turn to face our Human Resources Rep, Claire, standing in my doorway in her cute gray sweater and maroon skinny pants with pretty heels. Her red hair cascades down her back in loose waves like mine. Come to think of it there's a lot of us women working here with long hair. My old Boss must have had a thing for it. He hired all of us, but he's recently moved on to another branch of the agency in New York. Good for him, but I prefer it here in Florida where the weather is warm.

"Sorry to interrupt you. Looks like you were reading something good." She giggles and shifts her footing.

"Yyyyess. Oh my God, it's so good. Might have to send you this one."

"Please do. You know I love the naughty ones. So, I have news to share."

Leaning back in my chair I get cozy, readying myself for something juicy. "Do tell, sista."

Her toothy grin spreads wide before she lowers her voice. "You have a new Boss and he's hot-as-fuck."

Now my heart is racing. "What? When? Who? When does he start?"

She steps further into my office. "He starts today.

He's making his rounds now, introducing himself. Wait 'til you see him!"

My curiosity drives me to my feet and I peek around the door frame just as he steps up to my office door. Holy shit! It's Grayson Cole.

His blue-green gaze roams my body from top to bottom, lingers at my red heels then comes back up. "Emma?"

I stare at him in shock. My mouth is gaping open and the memories of masturbating to him two times, ok, seven times flashes through my mind and my cheeks get hot. "Grayson," I manage to say.

Claire's expression reveals her befuddlement. "You two know each other?"

"Yeah, we met about a month ago," he replies. His eyes still set on me, studying me.

I'm pretty sure my face now matches my red heels. That night was a combination of one of the sexiest and most embarrassing moments of my life. I wanted to call him, I really did, but my stupid phone. *Ugh! Mentally waves fist in air.* Now he probably thinks I wasn't interested or was too chicken to call.

"My phone broke," I blurt out.

Claire looks from one of us, to the other, then slips out the door.

"Your phone broke?" he asks questioningly.

Good God, I can't even think. He looks hot in his navy-blue suit, white collared shirt, silver watch, belt, matching pants, his shoes. Damn it! Why did I have to vomit on them that night?

"Yes, after you left I dropped my phone and lost all my new contacts."

He smirks. "Uh-huh."

What? He's not buying it. He even looks humored like I'm making this stuff up.

"Whatever did happen, I think it's best we keep that night between us. It's not something that the staff should know about."

Seriously, why does life not offer do-overs?

Awkwardly shifting my footing, I lean my butt against my desk. "I agree. So, should I call you Grayson, Mr. Cole, or Boss?"

My lip slides between my teeth. Mmm, Boss, I like the sound of that. I'd like to chant that while he bends me over his desk. Wait, no! Stop thinking like that. This guy is your Boss now! You need to take him seriously.

The mystery I remember seeing the night of the club glimmers in his eyes and his lips turn into a sexy grin. "Call me Grayson."

Are my thoughts that transparent? My cheeks grow warm. He probably knows what I was thinking.

My mind is so rattled right now, I can't even focus. I shake my head and pull my thoughts together. "Staff meeting. We should have one. That way, we can share our current projects and learn what you expect from us."

Adjusting his stance, Grayson straightens and clears his throat. "Yes. I'd like that. I'll send a staff email today for a meeting tomorrow. Do you think that's too soon?"

"No, not at all. As long as you're not the kind of Boss that drags on in meetings. Carl, our last Boss, liked to do that. We brought snacks to the meetings just so we could stay awake."

Grayson laughs and shakes his head. "I definitely don't drag on. I like to keep a steady, satisfying pace."

Shit! Words like that *do not* help my restless libido right now! And my face won't stop getting hot!

Grayson grins and that sexy smile tells me he's toying with me. Damn him!

"I understand you're the senior agent here? That means we'll be spending a lot of time working together. Can I rely on you to answer *all* of my questions until I'm fully up and running?"

All? There's a hint of ambiguity to his emphasis on all. "Yes, of course. Anything you need."

"I'm going to need a lot from you, Emma. I hope you're up for the challenge."

Grayson the panty-melter. That's what his name should be because what he just said disintegrated them. "I like to be challenged." Ok, that came out way too sexual.

The corner of his mouth raises and he nods. "I'm pleased you're on my staff, Emma. I'll let you get back to work." Grayson turns his back and looks over his shoulder before he disappears out the door. "Nice shoes, *Princess.*"

Oh! This man is trouble!

Claire comes rushing into my office as I take a

breath and uncomfortably adjust in my damp, little panties.

She closes the door behind her and folds her arms across her chest. "Start talking. How do you and Mr. Hottie know each other?"

I grind my teeth. "He asked me not to say."

Her eyes widen and she sucks in a breath. "Did you two sleep with each other?"

"No! I wish. I bet he's a beast in the bedroom. He's so sexy, controlled, and confident."

Claire giggles. "Your face is as red as your shoes."

"I believe it. He gets me all worked up." I grab paperwork off my desk and start fanning myself.

"So, what did happen if you didn't sleep with each other? I mean, there's obvious chemistry."

I purse my lips. "Can I share this with you, without it going *anywhere*? I mean *anywhere*. He's our new Boss and we need to respect him."

She rolls her eyes. "Duh! You know you can. If not for being the Human Resources Rep then as your best bud. Now get to sharing."

"A month ago, we met at club Sin and hit it off. The sparks were firing. We danced, made out, and I was ready to go home with him and sleep with him; then I got sick, threw up all over his shoes. He *still* gave me his number, which amazed me. I was like, this is the incredible kind of guy I'm looking for. *Then* my phone broke. I couldn't find him on social media. I was devastated. Haven't stopped thinking of him, then Bam! He's my new, hot Boss."

Claire leans against the door, smiling cheek-to-cheek. "Fate has handed you a second chance, Em. Don't mess this one up."

Dropping the stack of papers in my hand, I move around my desk and sit down in my chair in a huff. "Claire, he's my Boss now. That causes so many problems. You should know. You're HR!"

She laughs. "There's nothing in the company policy about employees being in relationships."

Leaning back, I cross my legs. "But if it doesn't work out, then we'll have an awkward Boss and ex relationship. What if it ends so badly that I'm miserable at work? You know how much I love my job and living here. I don't want to transfer. Besides, now that he's my Boss, he probably has zero interest in any relationship."

Claire juts out her bottom lip, then sucks it back in. "You don't know that and by the way he was looking at you, I'd say the interest is definitely still there."

I turn my head to the naughty manuscript on my screen then back to Claire. "Ugh! I need to get back to reading about this character's amazing sex life. My own sucks. I'll talk to you later."

LUNCH TIME ROLLS AROUND AND I've completed, *She Likes It Hot* and am left with a full on bookgasm. I'm gonna have to tell the author her book needs to be sold with either condoms or vibrators. It's cruel and unusual punishment to read it without either. Typing my thoughts into an email, I get it sent off to the author and offer representation. I feel so good each time I discover one. Authors send tens to hundreds of these kinds of queries and I'm sure when they finally get the response they've been waiting for, their whole world is changed, and I get to be a part of that. A smile raises the corner of my mouth as I hit send.

Another email goes out to Lisa, our level one Agent, who sent the manuscript to me. Only the truly good ones make it past her, to my inbox, where I decide whether or not to offer representation. The last email goes to Grayson, letting him know an offer for representation has been issued. The next step will be for him to issue the contract if the author accepts my offer. Carl always trusted my judgment and never questioned my offers, hopefully, Grayson will do the same.

Standing to stretch my legs and now starving for some nourishment, I open my office door and head to the lunchroom. My feet stop in their tracks. Grayson is in the center area, between offices, talking with Rachel. A knot tightens in my gut. Of all the women, she's one I don't want him talking to. Not that I have a say in who he talks to, but she's a man-eater. Gobbles them up and spits them out, one after another. She's a brunette too, although her hair is more auburn. She flicks it off her shoulder and pushes her double D's into his face. Of course he's looking at them. How can you not when they protrude from her body like two giant basketballs?

Granted, I have a nice rack myself, but I don't flaunt these puppies out there like she does. I at least keep them covered. This is supposed to be a professional setting, after all. She laughs and touches his arm. I almost want to hurl on his shoes all over again, just so I don't have to witness this. He smiles as he leans towards her. Gross! He actually seems interested in their conversation.

Clicking my heels a little too loudly, I stroll past them, giving my hips a little extra bounce. I glance over my shoulder and see his eyes move up to my face from my ass. Rachel's daggers are pointed at my back.

That's right, bitch. He's mine.

In the lunchroom, I place my chicken salad sandwich on my plate and open my smoothie. Grayson enters moments later, just as I'm about to carry it back to my office.

"Emma." He blocks the exit, standing in the frame of the door.

"Grayson, I see you've met Rachel."

Grayson studies me and I wonder what is going through his mind. "Mm, hmm. She's a nice girl. She sent me an offer she extended this morning."

"I just sent one, too, for *She Likes It Hot.*"

Grayson touches his watch, then adjusts it. "I'll take a look at it. Did you send me the manuscript?"

"I did. The author has a fast-paced, but detailed style. She sucks you into the world she creates and honestly, the sex scenes are smoking hot."

His mouth twists into a sexy grin. "I can't wait to take a look. It'll be good to learn what you like."

What I like? How about your face between my legs or doggie-style? Mmm, yeah, I'd like that. Oh jeez, Em. Pull it together.

Grayson steps closer, reducing the space between us and my body heats up. "I'd love to know what it is you're thinking every time your cheeks get red like that."

My nerves send a prickling sensation across my skin. Busted! "Mmm, some thoughts are best kept private."

"That good, huh?"

A chuckle slips out of my mouth. "Yes."

Grayson goes to speak, but then Rachel interrupts him. "Grayson, a few of us are going out to lunch. We'd love to take you out as a welcome to the agency. We're heading to Segarro's if you like their food."

Grayson turns, smiles appreciatively, then nods. "I'd love to." He turns to face me, looks at the food in my hand, then back to my face. "Emma, you should come too."

If for no other reason than to keep Rachel's mitts off Grayson, I decide to go. "Sure. Let me put this food away and then I'll extend the offer to everyone, unless you were excluding staff members for some reason." My gaze shoots to Rachel and she sneers when Grayson isn't looking.

"Of course not. The invitation is for everyone," she singsongs.

Bull shit, but nice save.

"We'll be heading out in five minutes," Rachel announces.

Grayson walks out and I hurry to put my food back in the fridge and rush to Claire's office for backup.

Claire shuts down her computer and gathers her purse. "Rachel's after him? I mean, I shouldn't be surprised, but I think his interest surprises me the most."

"He doesn't know her like we do. He's naive to her ways. Now hurry, I need to stop by my office and grab my stuff before she tries to leave without us."

Claire and I rush to my office. We make it to the lobby elevator, right as the doors are closing with it packed full of people including Grayson and Rachel. I see her snicker just before it shuts.

My lip curls. "No doubt she planned that one," I say to Claire.

"Of course she did."

We wait for the elevator to return and make it to the first floor lobby. Rachel is standing with her arms crossed, irritation on her face. Grayson is looking at us stepping out of the elevator and the rest of the staff is lingering and chatting with one another.

Grayson smiles at me as I approach. "Rachel said

she thought you weren't coming, but I thought we better wait, just in case."

I glance at Rachel, narrow my eyes, then smile at Grayson. "Thank you. That was very nice of you."

Together as a group, we walk the block to Segarro's. Rachel ensures she gets a seat next to Grayson. I take the one across from him. He looks to me. "What do you like to get here?"

"The Cuban sandwich."

Grayson closes the menu. "Sounds perfect."

The dark-haired waitress, wearing casual jeans and a pretty blouse, brings a tray with enough chips and salsa for all of us. "What would you like to drink?" she asks after placing them on our table.

We rattle off our drink and then lunch orders.

Grayson is watching me across the table and our eyes lock. He smiles warmly and I'm completely caught in his stunning gaze, remembering how incredible his lips felt when he kissed me. He nudges the salsa closer when I go to dip a chip and I smile. Rachel breaks our moment with her cutting voice.

"Grayson, what made you decide to work for the Schmidt and Costello Agency?"

Grayson's attention switches to Rachel. "I enjoy reading and particularly enjoy the business of representing authors in getting their work published. I've had my eye on Schmidt and Costello for a while and received some inside information about Carl's transfer. It felt like the right time to apply and make the move from a mid-size agency to a larger one." Grayson returns his attention to me. "It worked out. I'm satisfied with my choice so far."

Rachel eyes Grayson looking at me and snarls. I can't help smiling triumphantly. The rest of lunch continues with everyone asking Grayson questions and him returning questions about our job duties, current projects and getting to know each of us personally.

When the checks come, Rachel snags Grayson's. "We took you out today, so you're not paying."

Grayson gives a warm smile. It's clear he appreciated the gesture. "That's very nice of you."

And Rachel goes for the win. She talks Grayson up the entire walk back. I linger behind staring at his incredible ass and grimacing at the sound of Rachel's flirty laughter.

Claire elbows my arm. "Why don't you go up and talk to him?"

"Mmm, I'd rather not look desperate. Seeing it on Rachel shows me how sad it looks."

Claire burst out laughing and Grayson and Rachel glance back at us. I shrug with a mischievous grin on my face. Grayson smirks and Rachel narrows her eyes. It's a good thing she doesn't have disintegrating laser beams coming out of her eyes, like Cyclops, or I'd be split in two.

Back at the office, I close my door and bury myself in creating submission packets for publishers until Claire swings my door open, saying goodbye. "See ya, love. Don't stay too long."

I grumble something inaudible and she laughs and

closes the door. Pulling up my author spreadsheets, I update the rejections and requests to read. Lost in my work, I don't realize what time it is. Sometime later, my office door opens and glancing at the clock I see it's five-thirty, an hour past my time off. I glance over my shoulder to find Grayson watching me. "Why are you still here?" he asks with a frown.

"Mm, don't have anything to rush home to. At least here I'm doing something for someone."

I lean back in my chair as he enters farther into my office.

"Why don't you close up and we'll go have a drink."

I click my tongue against my cheek. "Remember how that went last time? It didn't work out too well. I ended up chucking all over your shoes."

Grayson laughs and the light, playful sound makes me smile.

"It was the most interesting first impression I'd ever seen."

Rolling my eyes, I shut down my projects and turn off the computer. "Yeah, that makes me feel *a lot* better."

Standing, I grab my purse and move toward him and my office door. He doesn't move and now I'm standing inches from him. His beautiful eyes stare into mine and I see something in his that brings my latent lust back to the surface.

"Did you really drop your phone?"

"I did. I wanted to call you, truly."

"I was disappointed when you didn't."

Fiddling with my fingers, I look away when the

tension builds, then return to meet his sensual gaze, making it harder to say what I'm thinking. "I guess it worked out the way it was supposed to because now you're my Boss."

The tips of his brows pinch inward. "That bothers you, that I'm your Boss?"

"It has the potential to cause problems down the road, you know, if we're intimate and it doesn't work out between us."

Raising his hand, Grayson brushes my hair behind my ear. His soft hand grazes my cheek, and I close my eyes, inhaling his incredible scent.

"You've thought of us then, being intimate?" His voice has taken on a sexual tone. I open my eyes. The same chemistry and desire we had at the club is radiating between us.

"I have." The words escape my mouth without thinking. It's like his need to know the truth from me is a string pulling the honest words from my lips.

Stepping closer to me, I can feel the warmth of his body. "I have too and I don't care that I'm your Boss."

"Grayson."

"Emma?"

Like a magnet pulling me in, I feel his lips meet mine. His lips are soft, his kiss seductive. My body buzzes to life, heat builds in my core, and I'm wet in a matter of seconds. He takes hold of my waist and then lowers his hand to my ass, pulling me against him as his other hand gets lost in my hair, gripping it in his fist as a sexual storm rages between our lips.

Pushed backward, my ass hits the desk and his hand reaches down, touches my thigh, then slowly raises my skirt. Rubbing his thumb over my underwear, he toys with my clit, making me moan into his mouth.

"You're so damn gorgeous. I want to take you here, now, Emma. I want to bend you over this desk and fuck you senseless."

Wanton need ripples through my body. I'm on fire, desirous throbbing in my ears, my pussy soaking wet for him. Licking the shell of my ear, his tongue dips in, then nibbles the lobe.

"Fuck me, I love that," I mumble aloud.

I can feel his lips smile against my ear. "Imagine what I can do when I have it on your clit."

My underwear is swept aside and a finger slides into me, then another. My orgasm starts to build and his mouth quiets the moans from my lips. In and out, he works me over the edge.

Behind us, a loud ring startles us both out of our daze. Its incessant ringing is like water dousing my sexual desire.

"Damn it!" Grayson removes his touch, reaches around me and hits the mute button.

My logical mind starts to work again and in my head, I'm chanting. *What are you doing? He's your Boss. Your Boss.*

"Grayson." I place my heels on the floor, pulling down my skirt. "I think we got carried away. We definitely need to slow things down."

Grayson nods. A bit of concern shows on his face. "Are you worried about others finding out?"

"That is a concern. I don't want them to think I'm sleeping with you for my own selfish interests."

"No one needs to know about us."

I swallow the lump in my throat. "I'm not interested in being a hidden thing on the side."

Grayson's expression morphs, becoming serious, agitated. "That's not what I meant."

"Even if you didn't. That's what it would be." I grab my purse from the desk. "It's time I get home. I'll see you tomorrow."

CHAPTER 3

EMMA

*W*HY?! WHY COULDN'T I JUST swallow my pride, have amazing sex, then come back to work the next day like nothing happened? Because dumb Emma has feelings, that's why. I want more than just sex with Grayson. I want it all. I want the kind of love I read in the sappy romance books. Wearing my lounge clothes, I land on my couch with a loud thump, waiting for Megan to arrive. Just as I'm getting cozy, she knocks. I amble to the door and swing it open.

"Trick or treat, let's eat this fucking sheet." Her lips are pulled back, revealing all her teeth in a crazy smile.

Uncontrollable laughter builds up in my gut and bursts out of my mouth. "You're nuts."

"And you love me still."

I take the bag from her and smile. "That I do. Did you get the garlic knots too?"

Throwing her jacket over the couch, she looks over her shoulder and frowns. "You even have to ask?"

Closing the door behind us, I go into the kitchen and set out the containers on the counter. She grabs two plates from my cupboard and a bottle of wine from the small wooden rack set back against the wall beneath the cupboards. She waves the bottle of Pinot Grigio at me.

"Yeah, that one."

With our plates full and our wine glasses topped off, we head into the living room. While I get cozy on the couch, Megan sets her food on the coffee table so she can look through the movies.

She pulls out two and holds them up in each hand. "So, which one is it gonna be? The Other Woman or How to Lose a Guy in 10 Days?"

I look at her and frown. "Really? It's like my life in both titles."

Megan bites her lip and fights back laughter. "So, your ex is an idiot. You'll find someone better. Maybe it's your Boss, who knows. Maybe it's someone else. My advice to you is to give into all your desires, have fun, don't hold back, and everything will work out the way it's supposed to."

"Damn, that's some good advice, Megs."

Popping open How to Lose a Guy in 10 Days, she puts it in the DVD player. "Well, you know, I am a genius."

Joining me on the couch, she takes her plate and dives into the spaghetti.

I glance at her and wink. "You think I should've given in to having sex with Grayson today? The truth is I don't want to *just be* a sexual relationship for him. I like him. I see potential for something real. If I give into a sexual relationship behind the scenes, why would he ever want more? What if I develop serious feelings and think we're more than we are? What if he starts seeing another woman?"

Megan slurps up a dangling noodle and her eyes widen. "Oh my God, Em, shut your brain off. You analyze way too much."

My lip pouts. "I know I do. It's probably why Derrick left me."

Megan grabs my wine glass off the coffee table and hands it to me. "Drink it. I can't take this self-deprecation anymore. You're in a funk and you need to get out of it. If you like Grayson, then just tell him you do."

After swallowing half the glass, I set it down and settle into my food and the movie. Maybe Megs is right, but why does the thought of telling Grayson I like him, completely terrify me? Probably because there's a chance at the end of it, he'll leave me too, and the wound from the last guy who did is still too fresh.

IT'S TUESDAY MORNING AND I may have dressed a bit sexier than my usual work attire in turquoise, lace-up stiletto pumps, a yellow, fitted, knee-high skirt, and a bit more revealing cream blouse. Standing in Claire's doorway, looking down, I admire my new pumps with her. We're both shoe whores, who have designated space in our closets for all the different pairs we own. Between our love of shoes and books, we instantly connected.

Her words trail off when we hear a couple co-workers, Tracy and Alexa, giggling beneath their breath. The giggling stops and I turn to see just who I expect, Grayson entering the office looking dashing in his gray suit, coral button-down, a silver metal bracelet on the opposite wrist than his watch and stylish, pointed, black shoes. Ugh! Will I ever again look at his shoes without thinking about that night?

Grayson doesn't make eye contact or say good morning to me like he does the others, but I know he's noticed me. He glances, deadpans, then continues on to his office. Yeah, that stung a bit.

I look to Claire. "Shit, I think he's upset."

Claire fusses with the end of her ponytail and leans back in her chair. "Better smooth that out the first chance you get."

I put a hand on the frame and lean back, peering at his office door. I almost slip and fall when he catches me looking and I try to pretend I wasn't. A moment later I hear him call my name across the lobby area.

Claire giggles. "Someone's in trouble. Maybe you'll get a *firm* reprimand."

Nibbling my lip, I roll my eyes at her and then gracefully walk to Grayson's office. When I enter, he motions for me to close the door. Nervously I do, then take one of the black leather seats in front of his desk.

Grayson looks at me and as hard as his jaw is set, his eyes are still soft as they stare at me.

"I read your notes on *She Likes It Hot*. I also read the first three chapters. I agree with you, it's a manuscript we can sell. I'd like to see what else you have. I want another three manuscripts by the end of the week."

A little surprised by the ambitious request, my lips part, and my expression likely shows my surprise.

"You can handle that, can't you? If not, I can see if Rachel is up for the challenge."

Irritation tickles my chest. "No, I can handle it. It's an adjustment is all."

A big adjustment. Carl was happy with one manuscript every week. Four in one week means longer hours at the office.

He nods, satisfied. "Good. I'll be scheduling a staff meeting at ten today to go over my expectations for everyone and to get the rundown on what projects are being worked."

His all-business attitude has me hoping it won't always be awkward between us.

"I'll be there."

Grayson looks away from me to his computer. "Thank you, Emma."

I let out a breath. There's no way I'm walking out of the office leaving this awkward tension.

"You're mad at me, aren't you?"

Grayson's attention returns to me. "I am, but I'm mostly upset with myself."

His honesty startles me. "Why?"

Grayson stands from his desk, moves to the glass windows of his office and touches them. They turn solid white and we can no longer see anything on the other side of them nor can anyone see in. With confident steps, he moves to his desk and sits on the edge, directly in front of me.

"I consider myself a patient man, but I think sometimes I like to fool myself into believing I am. For a month, I patiently waited to hear from you and when I didn't, I found myself surprisingly disappointed. Yesterday, you were put right in front of me, and all that time spent thinking of you got the best of me. I shouldn't have come on to you like that. You were right. I'm your Boss. I need to respect that and respect you. It won't happen again."

That was *not* what I was expecting. So much for telling him how I feel. "You didn't disrespect me."

Grayson gives me a forced smile and from there it feels like this conversation is coming to an awkward end. Scooting the chair back, I stand to leave. Grayson watches me as I go.

Before reaching the door, I stop and turn to him. I

want to say so many different things, but my voice catches in my throat. "I'll have the three other manuscripts to you by the end of the week." I open the door and walk out, feeling completely disappointed in myself.

God Emma, you are chicken.

My heels tap across the linoleum floor as I take a walk of shame back to my office. Once behind my closed door, I bury myself into a new book.

My calendar alarm goes off, reminding me of the 10 a.m. staff meeting. Prying myself away from the story I've been semi-sucked into, I open the door to find everyone bustling about, prepping for the staff meeting. As I enter the lunchroom, I see Rachel is already in there finishing off a yogurt.

A smirk smears her face as she watches me pour a new cup of coffee. "Did you hear Grayson accepted my manuscript? He said I have a real good eye for recognizing talent."

Hearing the compliment she received from Grayson irritates me. I ignore her and take a sip of the coffee.

She tosses her empty yogurt container into the trash. "Why do you look so bummed? Did Grayson turn down your manuscript submission?" She singsongs it in a hopeful tone.

"No, he accepted it," I reply with a curve of my lips. "He wants three more from me."

Rachel's mouth turns down. "He didn't ask for three more from me." She stares at me questioningly, as though I'm lying or did something special to get the request. *This* is exactly why I don't think a relationship with Grayson is a good idea.

"Don't fret, Rachel. You wouldn't want that pressure anyway. It would cut into your precious sex life."

Her expression goes from insulted to smug. "At least I have one. I heard about Derrick. Maybe if you spent less time reading about sex and actually doing it, he would've stuck around."

And with that, she saunters out of the lunchroom and I'm left standing there with a mixture of emotions coursing through me—anger, frustration, sadness, wondering if she's right, self-pity, then it all repeats.

Carrying my cute, polka dot coffee tumbler like a shield, I traipse into the staff room, taking a seat by the windows. Looking out over the town is a distraction as my eyes prickle with tears. Grayson enters and all the women straighten in their seats and push their breasts out in hopes of getting his attention. I barely turn my chair. He's the last person I want to face right now.

Grayson's voice carries through the room as he goes over his grand plans for the agency and how he envisions each of us taking part. Claire nudges my arm and I turn to face him. He's staring right at me, studying me as he continues to share ideas with the group. The women are enthusiastically wagging their tails at every word that comes out of his mouth. I set the coffee tumbler down and pretend to listen as my thoughts drift off into memories of Derrick and me in what used to be our apartment, our last Christmas, the last time we made love. When I feel the tears stinging in my eyes, I grab the tumbler and sip while trying to clear my mind.

Glancing up, I can see that Grayson is still watching me. He even seems concerned. A couple other women notice him staring and their attention centers on me. I cool my emotions and sit up straight, doing my best to seem engaged.

"I'd like to go around the room and each of you tell me your current projects and then that'll be it for today."

Lisa, my level one Agent, goes first and shares a few books she plans on sending me. I smile at her, encouraging a job well done, and am equally pleased to hear she has a couple romantic suspense novels and a romcom she wants to send. I'm in the mood for something less sappy. Too bad we don't accept thrillers because I'm not in the mood for reading romance.

Grayson dismisses everyone and Rachel lingers, using this as an opportunity to flirt. She says something funny and Grayson genuinely laughs. The way his eyes crinkle and his smile lights up his face sends warmth spreading through me and confuses me further. I rush to leave and I see in my peripheral he's watching me go.

Back in my office, I send several emails to authors and update my spreadsheets. A tap of knuckles on my door precedes Grayson as he comes in and closes the door. He takes a moment to look around my office and even glances at the photo of me and Megan on my desk.

"What's wrong?"

My gaze moves to the window. I look out at the nearby skyscrapers and the blazing sun casting a shadow from the building, while I regain control of my swirling emotions. "I'm fine," I reply, returning my attention to him.

His tone is disapproving. "You're not fine. Don't lie to me, Emma. I don't like to be lied to."

I chuckle at his demanding tone. "Well, if you must know. My ex of two years recently ended our relationship, moved out while I was at work, and then told me he was seeing someone else via text. Rachel did a great job reminding me of that today."

Grayson pauses in thought. His handsome face is expressionless, but I can tell the wheels are turning in that intelligent mind of his.

"How long ago?" he finally asks.

I lean back in my chair and cross my legs. Grayson's eyes follow the length of them, linger on my stiletto's, then return to my face.

"Two months ago," I reply.

"Huh, that's still fresh."

"That it is."

"What did Rachel say to you?"

Looking back at the computer, I refuse to reveal how much her comment affected me. "Doesn't matter."

The sound of Grayson's feet moving across the floor brings my attention back to him. He's standing close to my legs and even at that distance my heart rate increases.

"It matters to me. Tell me what she said." His jaw is set in determination. I'm not getting out of this.

My gut tightens, remembering the words. It's truly embarrassing. "She said maybe if I spent less time reading about sex and more time doing it, Derrick would've stuck around. Maybe she's right."

Grayson's expression remains emotionless, but his eyes are intense as they stare into mine.

"She doesn't know what the hell she's talking about. A man can have a stunning woman at home and still want what he can't have. Simply put, your ex is a dumbass for not realizing what an incredible woman you are."

A smile parts my lips. "That's nice. Thank you. Even though you're trying to make me feel better, it's still nice to hear it."

Grayson shakes his head. "That wasn't just to make you feel better. You know I'm attracted to you. I was from the first moment you fell into my arms."

My cheeks flush. "I should get back to work. Thanks for checking on me."

Grayson's jaw tenses, like it does every time he's irritated or has a change of emotion, then, without saying a word, he walks out of my office. Instead of reading, I stare out the window and daydream about how incredible it felt to be kissed and touched by Grayson Cole.

CHAPTER 4

EMMA

*I*T'S THE AFTERNOON AND I'M nearly finished with the second book I've read today. It's a sprint to the end now. Can't quit when I'm this close. I can't gobble the words fast enough. I'm on the edge of my seat and probably have red ink all over my lips from biting into my pen. A familiar tap raps on my door and I jump in my seat. Damn it! Five more minutes. That's all I needed! Glancing at the computer clock reveals I'm almost an hour past my time to be off.

Grayson peeks in and I notice he looks tired. "You're truly dedicated, Princess."

I chuckle and his tired expression lightens.

"Hard day?" I ask.

Grayson fully enters and closes the door. Moving comfortably about my office, he grabs a chair from the small table to the left, sets it next to my desk, then drops into it with one smooth, masculine movement. "Not hard, but mentally exhausting. I had several phone calls that lasted a while and took a lot of energy. I thought to myself when I left my office that if you were still here I'd offer that drink again. I think we both could use it."

It may not be the best idea to have a drink with Grayson, but he's clearly extending an olive branch for friendship, and honestly, what sane woman could say no to that sexy smile he's flashing at me right now.

"All right, a drink does sound good. Can you do me a favor, though?"

His smile curves in playful curiosity. "Anything for you."

"You're really putting on the charm, aren't you?"

He laughs but sounds serious when he speaks. "What can I do for you?"

"I'm less than five minutes from finishing this manuscript. You mind waiting while I read?"

He waves his hand and nods, indicating I should finish. "I know what that's like. There's no way I'm going to make you wait until tomorrow to finish."

A smile spreads across my lips. "Thank you."

Returning my attention to the manuscript, I slip back into the story within a few sentences. My red pen is back between my lips and I'm completely unaware that Grayson is watching me with an expression of contentment and fascination until I finish the last line and look over at him.

"Another good one, huh?"

Dropping my pen and taking a breath, I chuckle. "It

was. I'm going to offer the writer representation tomorrow."

I gather my things and stand at the same time Grayson does.

"Emma."

Hearing my name stops my movements. "Yeah?"

Grayson raises his hand, licks his thumb, and then brings his hand to my lips. With the touch of his damp finger he awakens my lust.

Standing so close, I can smell his intoxicating cologne. I close my eyes and breathe him in as his thumb rubs my lips. When he pulls his hand away, he's standing so close I can feel the warmth of his body. His jaw is set tight and his brows lowered. "You had ink on your lip."

"Yes, of course." I'm not even embarrassed. There's no room for it when my body is buzzing. Just the touch of his finger has my center warming to an undesirable level. With his blue-green eyes set on mine, I feel as though he wants to remove the space between us and give into the same thoughts I have, but instead, he clears his throat and takes a step back.

"We should get going."

There's a bar two doors down from our office building. With the evening sun descending into the sky, the breeze is cooler than earlier in the day. Walking into the breeze, I shiver from its cold embrace. Grayson brings his hand to my shoulder and gives one long, languid stroke across my back. His touch is warm and affectionate and that chill instantly dissipates from my body. With his hand removed, the chill begins to creep back, but we've made it to the entrance of Masco's and Grayson holds the door open for me.

Manners are something Grayson was definitely raised with. He knows how to treat a woman, and he continues to impress me when he pulls out a bar stool for me to sit before seating himself. The dark wood interior and low lighting make for a relaxed and intimate setting. In the background, instrumental music plays. The pepper-haired bartender, dressed in a button-down, white shirt, and black slacks, approaches with a smile.

"What can I get for you?"

"I'll take an Old Fashioned," Grayson tells him.

The bartender's attention turns to me. "And the lady?"

"A Sangria."

While the bartender moves about, preparing our drinks, Grayson focuses his attention on me. "What was the story you were reading this afternoon?"

"Romantic suspense. It's another we can sell. It's from an author we already represent. It's her third book and it's better than her first two."

"I look forward to your notes and reading some of it."

The bartender delivers our drinks and departs with a smile.

Taking a sip of the cool, refreshing liquid already has the tension from the workday easing away. "Do you ever read the manuscripts in full?"

"I do when I find it interesting enough."

"What's the last book you found interesting enough?"

"She Likes It Hot."

Warmth rushes to my cheeks. "You're reading the one I sent you?" I ask, completely surprised.

Grayson's mouth turns up, clearly humored by my reaction. "I am."

I'm blown away by his admission and a bit turned on. I know the contents of that book and it's not possible for someone to read it without getting heavily aroused. "What do you think of it?"

"It's as your notes said, erotically climatic."

I giggle sheepishly. "I said that, didn't I?"

"Made me want to read it, and the author's writing made me want to read more. After all, it is good to know what a woman likes."

The alcohol and conversation work together warming my body. I take another drink and hold back my smirk. A handsome man who likes to know how to please a woman. Grayson, the panty-melter, is disintegrating mine as we speak.

My silence seems to intrigue him.

"What are you thinking, Princess?"

My brow ticks. "Things that will get me in trouble."

"Now, Emma, don't tease me like that. I want to know everything you're thinking." His expression is playful, challenging.

If only he could see the images flashing through my mind. I don't have the gumption to say them out loud.

Grayson's hand tenderly places my hair behind my ear. "Emma, I like it when you're honest with me. I want you to always be honest." His thumb caresses my cheek, and his hand follows the shape of my chin before pulling back. That gentle and affectionate touch has my nipples hard against my bra and I adjust in my seat as the warmth builds at my core.

My lips part and with the alcohol giving me liquid courage, I start to speak.

"Grayson Cole."

My mouth snaps shut at the sound of his name coming from a tall woman with wavy, black hair, a red dress, and legs for days.

Grayson appears to recognize the voice, even without looking at her. His posture changes, going from relaxed to rigid, before turning to meet her gaze.

"Fancy meeting you here," she singsongs.

"Olivia. How are you?"

Her dark, brown gaze sweeps over me, taking in my looks, hair, clothing, then returns to him. "I'm very well. Here to meet a client for dinner and drinks. And you?"

Grayson motions to me. "This is my colleague and friend, Emma Williams. We're enjoying an after work drink."

Olivia extends her hand and gives a tight, quick handshake. "Pleasure." Her attention steadies on Grayson once again. "We should get together. It's been a while." The corner of her mouth raises into a flirty grin.

The underlying hint is clear, but Grayson doesn't acknowledge it. "Been busy with the new assignment. I'm working for Schmidt and Costello. When my schedule opens up, I'll try to give you a call."

"You should. I miss you."

She winks and my stomach churns. There's obvious history between the two of them and I'm sitting here like the awkward third wheel. I wave to the bartender for my bill.

When I look back at Olivia and Grayson, she's leaning in, whispering something in his ear with her hand on his leg. The other hand is stroking his neck and shoulder.

The bartender brings my bill and I reach into my purse, hand my credit card to him, hoping to scurry away from this awkward situation as fast as I can.

With my nerves making me clumsy, I smack the Sangria glass with my wrist as I pull back my hand. It topples over, clinks on the counter and the remaining bit of my drink pours out and onto Grayson.

"Shit!" I screech.

Grayson jolts from his stool as the cool liquid lands on his pants.

"Oh my God! I'm so sorry!"

Grabbing a wad of napkins, I pat at his pants and then stop as my cheeks burn red. I've just repeatedly smacked Grayson in the crotch and he's looking at me like I've lost my mind.

"It was an accident. I'm so sorry."

Grayson takes my wrist in his hand, removing the napkins. "It's okay, Emma."

"I'm gonna go. I'm so sorry. Send me the dry-cleaning bill. I'll see you tomorrow."

I rush out of the bar as fast as my heels will let my feet go.

As I lay on my bed, the palms of my hands are covering my face, as if it will diminish my embarrassment from dumping my drink all over Grayson's lap. Megan giggles in the background as she searches through my clothes. I don't even want to go out, but she's insisting we have dinner and drinks at this new comedy club she's been wanting to check out.

"Was it actually that bad? I mean, did you at least get to feel what he's packing?"

"No, I didn't even get that opportunity. I was too busy being horrified as I smacked the shit out of his crotch."

Meg's hysterical laughter echoes from my closet. "You're batting two to nothing with this guy. Twice now, you've embarrassed yourself by putting fluids on his clothing and not even the good kind."

She walks out of my closet carrying a fitted, black dress, with thick straps and black lace over the skirt part of the dress. "Here. I chose this."

"Oh, I like that one. It's one of my faves. I can wear it with my new, gold JS pumps."

In her pink, long skirt with a slit up to her upper thigh, and her black blouse tucked in, Megan looks curvy and killer. She put curls in her short, black hair and it frames her round face, making her look even more adorable than usual.

"Put it on and let's do your hair. We'll make the outside of you look so fabulous you'll forget how icky you feel on the inside."

Taking the dress from her hand, I set it on the bed while I undress. After sliding into it, we head into my bathroom and I turn on the curling iron. While she helps me pick out makeup and I put loose curls in my hair, I listen to her talk about her day.

We're finished, looking fabulous and about to walk out the door when a knock startles us. Reaching for the door, I open it and my jaw drops. Grayson is standing on the outside in dark, denim jeans, a maroon, long-sleeve sweater, and stylish black shoes. His hair is going every which way and he looks freshly showered. I can smell him from where I'm standing and his masculine scent is already making my thighs rub together.

"Emma." His tone sounds surprised.

I'm equally taken aback to see him at my door. "How'd you find...never mind, you have my files."

Looking at my dress, then shoes, he brings his attention back to my face. "I had to stop by the office to get the address, so I could bring you this." Grayson raises his hand, and in it, is my credit card.

He must think I'm an absolute moron at this point.

"Thank you so much for bringing it by." My cheeks are warm as I take it from his outstretched hand.

"I would have waited until tomorrow to give it back to you, but I had a feeling you might need it for dinner. I remember you said you like to have dinner out."

Megs nudges my arm as butterflies flap around in my belly. I'm enamored with the fact he remembered that detail about me.

"Oh, Grayson this is my best friend, Megan. The one who was with me that night at Sin. Megan this is…" I pause. For some reason the words, *my Boss*, sound so impersonal and Grayson and I may not be anything special to each other, but whatever we are, it's more than just a Boss and employee. "Grayson," I finish.

He reaches out and Megan takes his hand to shake. "Pleasure to meet you, Megan. It's nice to know someone so important to Emma."

"Nice to meet you too."

His attention settles back on me. There's a spark of something in his eyes as he stares, admiring me. "You look gorgeous, Emma. Where are you headed?"

"We're going to La Rosa Comedy Park," Megan shares, then looks to me. "I'll meet you downstairs in the car."

Grayson steps out of the way as she passes.

"I'm so sorry about dumping my drink on you earlier. I meant it, I'll pay for the dry cleaning."

The slight curve of his lips lightens his eyes. "Don't worry about it. It's me who owes you an apology. You wouldn't have spilled it if you hadn't been uncomfortable in that situation. I'm sorry I made you feel that way."

"It's ok. It was time for me to go. I feel bad for interrupting things between you and Olivia." *Lies, all lies, Em. And he told you he likes it when you're honest with him.*

"Are you sure about that?"

Why did he have to ask?

"No," I admit.

A smile lifts the corner of his mouth and he runs his tongue across his bottom lip. That little movement turns the inferno in my vagina up a notch.

"Emma." He takes a couple steps, closing the distance between us. "Olivia doesn't mean anything to me. She's an ex-girlfriend. We parted on amicable terms."

"You mean you became friends with benefits?"

A light chuckle escapes him. "Yes."

"Are you still friends with benefits?"

"No. Would it bother you if we were?" His eyes study mine, awaiting my response.

I swallow and lower my head, not wanting to admit that it would.

A gentle touch of his hand lifts my chin to meet his captivating gaze. "Tell me the truth."

"Yes," I whisper. "It would."

Placing his hand on my cheek, he holds me steady as he kisses me. The touch of his lips turns my whole body into a scorching inferno. His other hand takes hold of my hip and pulls me against his body. With tender movements of his lips, all my thoughts go blank as I'm filled with a sensuous, utterly mesmerizing euphoria.

When he takes his lips away, I lean into his embrace.

"You look stunning in this dress and those fuck-me-heels. Be careful tonight. You're going to draw a lot of attention."

His thumb grazes across my lips and with a peck on my cheek, he leaves.

Barely able to form a thought, I stroll down to Megan's car. I get in, still in a daze and she giggles.

"What happened to you?"

"He kissed me."

"And?"

"His lips are like cinnamon and chocolate. Hot *and* delicious."

Laughing, Megan starts the car. "You're such a dork. Well, what now?"

"I don't know. We'll see what happens tomorrow."

Megan drives off to the comedy club and my thoughts are still up in my apartment as the tingling memory of his kiss torments me.

CHAPTER 5

EMMA

*W*HEN I WALK INTO MY office, my eyes dart to the single, white rose lying on my keyboard. There's no note, but I know who it's from. After setting down my purse and turning on my computer, I pick up the rose and with a girlish grin, I open my office door to go thank Grayson.

As I approach his office door the glass windows are shaded white; he's clearly busy. I turn on my heels, but then the office door opens and with a giant smirk on her face, Rachel waltzes out. Her eyes mock me as she sways her hips and saunters away.

Like painful indigestion, jealousy forms an irritating ball in my chest. Opening the door to Grayson's office, I find him settling back in his seat with a stack of papers.

"What was she doing in here with the windows shaded?"

Grayson's gaze raises to mine and I shudder. Wow, that

came out sounding crazy jealous and I'm not even his girlfriend!

"Good Morning to you too, Emma."

"I'm sorry. I—"

"Was jealous," he finishes, grinning.

I let out a huff. "Yes."

"Why are you jealous?"

"She has the hots for you and Rachel goes after what she wants."

"Why don't you?"

Embarrassed, feeling like I've been put on the spot, I fiddle with the rose in my hand. "Life isn't like the romance books. It doesn't all end in a fairy tale."

With the tightening of his jaw, Grayson stands and approaches me. He takes the rose from my hand and with a slow, confident movement he brushes my hair off my shoulder. "Close your eyes for me, Emma."

With nerves igniting throughout my body, I close my eyes and await with anticipation.

Just below my ear, a tender kiss meets my neck and I shiver with heightened arousal.

"All you have to do is learn to trust again." His breath is warm on my ear, followed by the slow, sensuous touch of his tongue on my skin. He nips at me as the rose touches between the cleavage of my breasts. "Do you trust me, Emma?" His tone is confident, unhesitating, and my body yields to that self-assurance.

"Yes," I breathe.

For a moment, there's no contact and my body

yearns for his touch. Just when I'm about to say something, I feel his hand on the inside of my thigh. "If you trust me, Emma, let go of any reservations."

"Grayson," I whisper, but his name trails off as his lips cover mine.

Sliding his hand under my skirt, he finds my panties. Adding his other hand, he raises my skirt up my thighs and puts both hands on the straps of my underwear. As my skin tingles with desire, he slides them off my hips. Lowering himself, he caresses down my leg. Gentle kisses are placed along my calf before he lifts my heel and has me step out of my panties, one leg after the other.

He slides my black, lace underwear into his pocket and a devilishly, handsome smirk tilts his mouth as he stares into my eyes. "I didn't tell you to open your eyes, Princess."

Biting my lip, I close my eyelids. His tongue slips between my lips and unleashes the ravenous need within me. His hand trails up my thigh once more, finding me soaking wet for him.

A satisfied breath escapes his lips. "You're ready for much more than I can give you now, Emma."

Two fingers massage my clit and my head rolls back as my nipples harden and a wave of pleasure courses through me. His body moves closer and a hand takes hold of my lower back. The pressure on my back tightens as his strokes move in a faster rhythm.

The tip of his tongue licks the shell of my ear, then sucks it into his mouth. Letting out a desperate moan, I can feel him smile against my ear. "Today, I want you to think about how good it will feel to have me inside you. Tonight, I want you to give into that desire."

His lips sweep across mine before his tongue slides between my mouth. My moan is muffled by his kiss as my orgasm explodes and ripples through my body.

NOTHING LIKE A MORNING ORGASM from your Boss. Yeah, that shit just happened. After a little clean-up in the bathroom, and firing a *holy shit* text off to Megan, I squeeze my legs together as the memory of the hot-as-fuck scene in his office replays through my mind. Grayson Cole, upgraded from panty-melter to panty-stealer.

My door flies open and Claire rushes in. Closing it behind her, she gives me a pointed look. "Start talking."

"Hmm?" I play coy.

"Rachel is starting a rumor that you're both fucking Grayson."

Wait, what? That's not what I expected her to say. "Rachel said she slept with him?"

"That's what she's saying. She said you were sloppy seconds."

I feel like I've been punched in the stomach.

"Is it true?" she asks, concerned.

"I…didn't know he slept with Rachel." Tears prickle my eyes. "No, I didn't sleep with him."

"Oh love, I'm sorry." She moves in for a hug as a tear rolls down my cheek.

I wipe away the tear and wrap my arms around her.

"You want to go for an early lunch?"

Pulling my arms back, I nod. "Yeah, I don't feel like being here right now."

When I walk out, Grayson is in the lobby talking with Rachel and Tracy. Rachel looks at me and smirks. Grayson sees me and raises his head to get a better look at me. I turn away from both of them and walk out with Claire.

Lunch at Segarro's doesn't help. I can barely eat, feeling like a fool for letting myself feel anything for Grayson. Just like the saying; early bird catches the worm. Rachel caught it alright and probably gave it an STD while she was at it.

"Stupid cunt," I blurt out.

"Damn, Em, you're pissed about this, aren't you?" Claire asks, her brown eyes wide.

"I should've known. Rachel sleeps with anything that has a penis in a ten-mile radius. I guess I thought there might've been something between Grayson and me."

Claire juts out her bottom lip. "I'm sorry, Em. I don't know what to say. I know this is exactly why you didn't want to get involved in the first place. You aren't going to leave and take another job, are you?"

I shake my head. "No, I'll have to suck it up and get over it. From now on, it's all business, though. I'm gonna take the rest of the day off and work from home. Will you tell Grayson I wasn't feeling well?"

"Yeah, I can do that."

"Thank you."

After paying my bill and saying goodbye, I head straight home. The first thing I do is take a shower, washing off any remaining memory of Grayson and our morning session. With comfy, pink shorts, a tank top, and my fluffy, cream slippers, I create a makeshift desk on my coffee table, open up my laptop, and get to work.

A couple hours into a book I doze off. The sound of hard knocking at my door startles me awake. I rub my eyes as I amble to the door. Grayson, still in his work clothes, is on the other side, staring at me with what looks like a mixture of worry and confusion.

"Are you actually sick?"

"What time is it?"

"Four-thirty. I came straight here. Are you okay? Claire told me you went home because you weren't feeling well. Is that true?"

"It is." Truthfully it is, but not for the reason he thinks.

"Can I come in?"

"I don't think that's a good idea."

His jaw tenses. "I'm not worried about getting sick, Emma."

"I'm not sick, Grayson. I'm disgusted."

Oh shit, can't take that back.

He grimaces, clearly confused, maybe even a little angry. "*Why* are you disgusted?"

"It's my own fault. I didn't ask this morning if anything had happened between you and Rachel. Foolish me believed you're a nice guy. That you were actually into me, well *just* me anyway. Unfortunately, I heard about you and Rachel having sex after you had already stolen my underwear."

Grayson glares at me. Oh, yes, he's definitely pissed.

Pushing through my doorway, Grayson enters and closes the door behind him. "Emma." He stalks toward me, quickly eliminating the space between us. I back up until my ass hits the couch. Grayson lifts me, sets me on the back of the couch, enters between my spread legs and gets close enough I can smell his sinful cologne. "I don't give a fuck about Rachel and I *didn't* fuck her either. I don't know how much clearer to make it. You're the only woman I want to stick my dick in."

My jaw drops and I stare at Grayson as a mixture of emotions tumbles around in my belly. "You didn't sleep with Rachel?"

"I wouldn't touch her with my eight-inch pole, but it didn't stop her from trying. Yes, this morning she made advances. Advances that I could easily fire her for, but I'm not looking to make her jobless just because she was interested in a romp in the sack. I made it clear it wouldn't be happening. I have no doubt she got pissed off when you walked in with a rose and came back out with a satisfied grin. She took a low blow at you, and you fell for it."

"You really have an eight-inch pole?"

The corner of his mouth curves. "Emma, is that all you heard?"

A playful giggle escapes me. "No, but it sure did stand out among all the words you just said."

"Now you're thinking about how much you want to see it, aren't you?"

Nibbling on my lip, I glance down at his zipper, then back to his face. "I am."

Grayson grabs my ass and tugs me against him. "Too damn bad. I'm going home."

"What? Why?"

He drops my legs and I stand. He's backed away and I already miss the contact of his warm body.

"You should've come and talked to me, Princess, and not believed the rumor."

"Grayson, I'm sorry."

"When you're ready to trust me, I'll show you how appreciative I can be."

Without another word, he walks out of my apartment.

CHAPTER 6

*W*ALKING INTO MY OFFICE THE next morning, I find a white rose is laying on my keyboard. I smile and add it to the one already in the vase on my desk. Today there's something with the rose. I pick up the tickets and read them—theater tickets to a romance show, Dirty Dancing. At first, I wonder how he knew I'd be interested, but then again, I'm a romance agent. I love all things romance. Placing the tickets in my purse, I stroll over to his office.

The windows are white, but the door is cracked open. I peek in and see him sitting in a sharp, navy-blue suit that accents his stunning blue-green eyes, focused on the computer screen.

"Is it okay if I come in?"

A charming smile parts his lips. "Yes, come in."

I close the door behind me and walk to his desk. "I got the tickets and the rose. I happily accept your invitation."

Grayson leans back in his chair, looks over my silver blouse, red skirt, and black heels. "Come here."

With a few steps, I'm standing in front of him and his chair.

"Sit in my lap, Emma."

"What if someone walks in?"

"Do I look concerned?"

Taking my hand, he pulls me onto his lap. I giggle and he covers the sound with a kiss. His hand snakes up my skirt, caressing me. I moan into his mouth and his kiss deepens.

"Does this mean you're no longer mad at me?" I ask between his arousing strokes.

"I was over it the moment I walked out of your apartment, but you needed to learn I take trust serious."

One finger slides into me, then another and I push against him as my breath quickens. "Grayson, what if someone walks—oh my God, that feels so good."

His thumb pinches my clit as his fingers work inside me. Pulling my body against his chest, his tongue whips along my ear and nibbles down my neck. "You want me to stop?"

"No, your fingers are fucking magic."

Grayson chuckles into my ear. "You're incredibly sexy when you're about to come."

I smile as I lean my head against his cheek, my body warming with my oncoming orgasm. His strokes become rhythmic, moving steadily, pulling my orgasm to the surface.

"Grayson, I'm going to—"

My body trembles in his arms as I reach my release.

Turning my face to him, I kiss him with passionate need. I rest my head against his and see a satisfied smile on his face.

"I'm tempted to take these panties too." Tugging at the straps playfully, he winks.

"You can't have them all."

He stares me down, challenging me. "Yes, I can. Knowing you're walking around the office without any, turns me on."

Leaving his lap, I stand, slowly lift my skirt, pull down my silky, strappy underwear and place them in his hand. He opens his drawer, puts them in and with a grin he stands and kisses me.

"Time to get back to work, Princess."

I turn to leave and he takes hold of my waist and pulls me back against his chest. His heated breath and damp lips caress my neck. Against my ass is his hardened erection. "Not without one last kiss." Turning me to face him, he pushes me against his desk and with his hand lost in my hair he ends our time together with a sensual kiss.

I leave his office in a sexual daze. Thankfully, the only person who sees me is Claire as she's walking to the lunchroom. She studies me and my expression as I pass the lunchroom on my way to the bathroom. I know she'll be in my office in a matter of minutes wanting to know every detail.

My office door opening behind me brings warmth to my cheeks. I turn in my chair and lean back, smiling at the questioning look on Claire's face.

"Last time we spoke you were upset that Grayson and Rachel were sleeping together, now you're walking around with a Cheshire cat grin. What's going on?"

"He didn't sleep with Rachel. She lied to upset me."

Claire crosses her arms and her expression is serious, worried even. "Are you sure? What if Grayson is lying?"

Crossing my legs, I set my pen down. "He's not. Grayson takes honesty and trust very serious. He made it clear she made a pass and he wasn't interested."

Uncrossing her arms, she steps up to my desk and leans over to smell the roses. "You are the only one he's getting flowers for. I see him bring it in every morning and put it in your office. It's so sweet." Her finger grazes the rose petals as she smiles at me. "Why white though? Why not red?"

My brows turn down as I lean forward and touch the petals myself. "I'm not sure. I'll have to ask him. What I know about white roses are that they symbolize purity and innocence and traditionally they were the symbol of true love before the red rose. Both baffle me because I'm neither pure, nor innocent and we're definitely not in the *I love you* stage, but I do love them. They're stunning."

Claire turns toward my office door. "Let me know what he says. I'm interested to know the answer."

Looking over her shoulder, she turns back to face me with a curious expression. "What happened in his office this morning?"

My cheeks flush and her eyes widen. "Did you guys have sex?"

Chuckling, I shake my head. "No."

"Are you going to tell me what did happen, cause your cheeks are as bright as your skirt."

"No, I'm not," I reply with a grin.

"Are you serious? You two have a hot office romance going on and you're not going to share anything with me?"

"I don't think Grayson would like it if you knew."

"That good?"

"Yeah, it's pretty juicy."

Claire throws her hands in the air. "You better send me a hot manuscript to make up for this."

"I have just the one."

"Good." Claire flashes a smile, then leaves.

Just after she walks out, my phone plays a jingle, alerting me to a text. I raise it and look at the screen. It's a new number I don't recognize. I open it and read.

I have something that belongs to you, Princess.

Immediately a smile swells my cheeks.

Going through my files again?

I've learned a lot from them.

Like what?

You're 28, beautiful, and well-educated.

My files say I'm beautiful?

I've updated them to reflect my observations.

What else have you observed?

You have a habit of stealing time while at work.

What do you mean?!

I spend half my time thinking about you in those heels and nothing else. You're taking away time I should spend working.

Clever :)

I am. Perhaps you should update my files with your observations.

Would love to. Has an 8-inch pole, magic fingers, and smells like sin.

You haven't actually seen the 8-inch pole.

We can rectify that.

We will.

My office phone rings and I set my cell phone aside, grinning from ear-to-ear with butterflies fluttering in my belly.

It's one of the authors I represent and she has a barrage of questions. I answer the ones I can and take notes to follow up on the others. Ten minutes later, I hang up and glance back at my phone. There are no new texts and I pout. Clicking on his number, I hit save and enter his name with the added title—the panty-stealer.

I'T'S FIVE MINUTES UNTIL THE time I'm off work and this whole day without panties has been a constant reminder of our sexy morning rendezvous. Anxious to go on our date, I'm rushing to finish off my last email. When I hear the door open, I'm too focused to look up. Strong hands pull my hair back from my face, then begin massaging my neck and shoulders. A smile parts my lips as I hit send.

"That feels amazing." My muscles relax and my posture goes slack.

"Looking forward to tonight?" he asks, his voice smooth.

"I am. Are we having dinner before?"

"We are. I'll pick you up at five-thirty." The massaging stops and his lips feather along my ear, sending goose bumps across my skin. "I might have to fire you, Princess."

I smirk. "Why's that?"

"I couldn't get anything accomplished with you on my mind."

His fingers tangle in my hair, then tighten, and tilt my head to the side. Erotic kisses travel up and down my neck. Reaching my ear, he licks along the shell, then nibbles my lobe. My nipples become pointed peaks and my breathing grows deeper.

"Grayson." His name is a whispered plea for more.

"Five-thirty, Princess. Don't wear any panties tonight, unless you want me to take them, too."

Placing one last kiss on my neck, he departs, leaving me yearning for more.

CHAPTER 7

*A*FTER A SHOWER AND GETTING dressed in one of my sexiest, black dresses—fitted, short, with lace sleeves, and just the right amount of cleavage—I slip into my tie-up, black stilettos. I leave my naturally wavy, dark hair loose and cascading down my back. I put on a smoky eye shadow to match my gray eyes. A look in the mirror leaves me feeling incredibly sexy.

The familiar tap of knuckles on my door echoes into my room. I hurry to the door, excited for Grayson to see me. When I open the door, his eyes widen, and he slowly admires my outfit, head-to-toe.

"Emma, you look stunning."

He enters, closing the door behind him. I admire him in his perfectly fit black suit, styled hair, and sexy-as-fuck smile that's still gleaming as he looks at me.

"We have a problem," he says, his expression serious.

"What problem?" I ask, concerned.

"Remember how I said I believe I'm patient?"

"Yes."

"I'm struggling with patience right now, with you looking like this."

I'm pulled into his arms and kissed. Beneath his lips, I feel his restrained, sexual tension. With firm, roaming hands, he caresses down my back and lower to my ass, pressing my pelvis flush against his.

"Emma, please tell me there's nothing under this dress."

A smirk widens my mouth. "There's not."

A wicked smile forms as he lets out a satisfied groan. "Come on, Princess, before we miss our reservation."

Aqua may be a silly name for a restaurant, but it is one of the most popular in town and difficult to get into. After the valet takes Grayson's sleek, silver, sports car, his hand finds its way to my lower back as he guides me into the restaurant.

Behind the hostess station is a woman near my age with pretty blond ringlets, red lips and a black blouse with matching black dress pants. "Mr. Cole, we've been expecting you. Right this way."

I'm a little startled she recognized him and Grayson smiles at me as if to reassure me it's not an intimate recognition.

Pulling my chair out, Grayson waits for me to sit. As he takes his seat, I get a good look at the restaurant I've never had the pleasure of being inside of. The large, glass windows overlook the lights of the city and just outside is a pond with a brightly lit fountain at the center. Inside, each round, glass table has a small aquarium in the middle, housing a beautifully colored Siamese fighting fish. Dangling from the ceiling are blue lights that give the restaurant an aquatic ambiance. The bar is also glass, with stunning salt water fish swimming inside the front of it.

"This place is amazing."

Grayson's eyes express his satisfaction as he watches me admiring all the details like a kid in a candy store.

"I thought the same thing the first time I came here. It's one of my favorite restaurants in town."

"How'd you get a reservation so quickly? I heard reservations book out more than a week in advance."

"My father and I have been coming here for years."

It's the first time Grayson has mentioned anything personal about himself. I jump at the opportunity to discuss more but am interrupted by the waitress.

With sparkly eyes and glossy lips, her brown hair is pulled back, and she's wearing a similar uniform as the hostess. "Mr. Cole, a pleasure to see you again." She fills our glasses with water, then smiles, and looks at me. "My name is Sarah. What can I get you to drink?"

Apparently, she doesn't need to ask Grayson what he wants. "I'll take a blackberry Mojito."

"I'll have that here for you in a moment." After rattling off the Chef's special, Sarah disappears to get our drinks.

Once I finish looking over the menu, my attention returns to Grayson. "I get the impression you're some kind celebrity here. Are you a rich bachelor and I don't know it?"

Grayson chuckles. "My father is just that. He's a well-known and wealthy bachelor in town—Arnold Cole."

"Your father is the owner of Cole Industries?"

Grayson nods. "I've kept my life separate from his, but Aqua is a place we frequent when we get together."

"Any siblings?"

Grayson shakes his head.

"Are you in contact with your mother?"

His jaw ticks like it does when he's irritated or has a change of emotion, but I can't identify which it is. Again, he shakes his head and thankfully, the awkward tension is disrupted by Sarah bringing us our drinks.

"Your Old Fashioned, Mr. Cole and your Mojito," she says, setting the glass close to me. "Have we decided on what to order?"

Grayson looks to me.

"I'll have the Salmon Béarnaise," I reply.

"Great choice," she tells me.

"The Prime Bone-in Filet," Grayson says, followed with a cordial nod.

"Thank you, Mr. Cole. I'll have your dinner out to you both shortly."

She disappears again and Grayson's attention settles on me as he takes a drink. "Ready for the show tonight?"

"I am. It's one I've wanted to see, but haven't had the chance to go; plus, Megs isn't into anything romantic, and Claire is married and always busy with her husband and daughter."

"I'm pleased I'm the one who gets to take you."

There he goes again, charming me with his words. "Me too. Would you normally watch this kind of show or are you doing it for me?"

"For you, but I'm sure I'll be entertained."

And now the question I've been dying to know. "The white roses you've been leaving me, I adore them, but I'm wondering what they symbolize to you."

Unbuttoning his jacket, Grayson relaxes into his chair, never taking his eyes off me. "In the Victorian Era, men would bring women a bouquet of white roses to symbolize they intended to pursue the woman in courtship."

"Does that mean you intend to *court* me?" I giggle.

"I do and I am."

"You're quite the romantic, Grayson Cole. You drink Old Fashioned, take women to romantic plays, and know about Victorian Era traditions. No wonder you're an agent of romance novels."

His smile tells me he's humored by my statement. "I told you it's good to know what a woman likes."

My curiosity is piqued. "Why is that?"

Beneath his eyes is that mystery I still have yet to discover. Grayson is a romantic, but he's also very private. I feel there's so much more to discover about him and that I've barely scratched the surface.

Sarah approaches our table and Grayson smiles pleasantly as she sets our plates down.

"Enjoy."

She departs and after my first bite, Grayson asks how it is.

"It's perfect. Incredibly delicious."

Grayson gives me that handsome smile of his and like a lovesick fool, I'm full of bubbles and butterflies on the inside.

"Good, I hoped you'd like the food here."

Conversation slows as we eat our meals. A while later, Sarah takes the empty plates and offers dessert.

I wave my hand. "No, thank you. The meal was perfect. No room left."

Sarah nods and scurries off.

"Maybe after the show, you'll want dessert. I know a place we can pick up something sweet."

Taking my napkin from my lap, I set it on the table. "Sounds perfect."

Sarah returns and brings the bill and Grayson quickly pays. With a glance at the bill, my eyes widen. One meal at this place is what I spend on two weeks of groceries and on top of it, Grayson gives Sarah a very large tip. I swallow the lump in my throat at how much he just spent on me.

"Thank you, Mr. Cole. Hope to see you again."

Raising to my feet, I move into Grayson's arm when he extends it around me.

"Thank you. That was the best dinner I've ever had."

With a gentle graze of his lips, he kisses my head. "I'm glad you enjoyed it."

The valet delivers Grayson's car and opens the door for me. Once I'm in, Grayson speeds off to the theater.

I twiddle my fingers as I think about the cost of the meal we just had. "I've never had a man spend that much money on me, Grayson. I appreciate it and admittedly feel bad that you spent so much."

Grayson glances over at me and the corner of his mouth raises. "Don't you know you're not supposed to look at the bill?" His hand moves up and grazes my jaw. "You're worth it, Princess."

I don't know if it's the fact that I'd just spent the last two years being madly in love with Derrick just to have him rip my heart out, but my brows tighten and I ask, "Why am I worth it?"

Grayson seems taken back by the question. "Emma, you shouldn't have to ask. You're beautiful, intelligent, independent, funny, and sexy-as-hell when you moan."

My cheeks warm from the memories of our morning escapades. I spend the rest of the ride wondering what is happening between Grayson and me and whether or not I can trust him like he wants me to.

Driving into the parking garage, he finds a spot then comes to my door and opens it. When I get out, his hand cups my cheek and he moves me against the car, pinning me between him and it. His warm body presses into mine, his hand tangles in my hair and gives it a tug. The tingling pain mixes with the pleasure of his kiss.

Leaning back, he looks into my eyes and his soften. "I appreciate that you're genuinely grateful for the dinner. You're the first woman to be humble about the gesture."

Surprised, I angle my head. "What kind of women do you normally date?" I immediately think of Olivia. "Never mind. I'm guessing they're all beautiful, intelligent, and independent women. You have a type, don't you?"

Grayson takes my hand in his as we walk to the theater. "I do."

"Am I your normal type?"

Grayson looks at me and winks. "You're a little different."

"Good different?"

"Yes, Emma, good different."

A giant smile spreads across my face as we walk into the lavish theater.

CHAPTER 8

*T*HE DIRTY DANCING SHOW WAS amazing and I even got teary-eyed at the end from its sheer awesomeness. Grayson takes my hand as I stand with him to leave.

"I have to admit, that was better than I expected," he shares.

"Oh my God, right?! That was incredible. Loved the end as much as I love the end of the movie. Great finale. I'm glad you brought me. Thank you." I turn to face Grayson in the throughway of the theater and kiss him.

He doesn't care that people are walking past us. He deepens the kiss and my body ignites.

"Grayson," his name is a needy whisper.

Captivating blue-green eyes lock on mine. "I think we should forgo dessert, Emma. There's something I'd like to have instead."

"What?" I ask coyly.

Grayson's mouth tilts into a grin. "You, Princess."

To my surprise, Grayson doesn't drive to my apartment. I quickly realize he's taken another route and I assume it's the route to his place. When we get there, I'm not shocked to see that it's a condominium in the upscale part of town. Pulling into a private parking garage, he comes to my side of the car and opens the door for me.

When I step out, he affectionately strokes my hair away from my face and then kisses me. "I brought you to my place. Is that okay?"

After I nod, I can see satisfaction fill his eyes. He takes my hand and leads me to the elevator. Six floors up and we walk into a small lobby that leads to three hallways—one left, one right, the other straight ahead. Taking the straight hallway, we reach his door a way down on the left side.

With the door opened, he motions for me to enter first. I do and I'm blown away at how stylish his apartment is. There's custom built wooden shelves on the right wall above the living room furniture, filled with different books. Below the shelves is a black suede couch, plush rug, and a large TV in the corner of the wall that partially separates the living room from the entryway. To the left is a black and metal breakfast table and beyond that, a kitchen that's made of dark wood and steel, with matching silver appliances. The kitchen has beautiful dangling yellow lights that match the single one dangling in the living room. A wide hallway cuts through the center and leads to what I assume are the bedrooms and bathroom.

"Your condo is gorgeous."

"I knew you'd like it."

My gaze is fixed on the shelves, admiring them. "You know my favorite part is the custom shelves with all the books, right?"

Removing his jacket, Grayson hangs it on a multi-peg hanger fastened to the wall next to where I'm standing.

"I do. It's my favorite too. Although, there is something else I like just as much."

I fully turn to face him, very interested in what it is.

Grayson takes my hand and nods his head. "I'll show you."

The warmth of his hand holding mine brings me such comfort it alarms me. Each time he takes it I don't want him to let go and I know that means I'm developing a deeper connection with him. With a deeper connection comes feelings, and with feelings, the opportunity for heartbreak.

While he leads me down the hall, I take in the beautiful painting that nearly fills the wall. Colors are strewn every which way, taking your eyes in different directions, and each new place you look, there's a new detail to discover. We pass a door along that same wall and I get a quick glimpse of what looks like a home office done in dark wood furniture and filled with more books.

Turning the corner takes us to what looks like his

bedroom. Entering, I'm mesmerized by the beauty outside of the floor-to-ceiling windows. The cityscape is just beyond the clear glass. Layers of black and silver buildings showcase bold, bright lights. Above, the nearly full moon cascades a soft hue into his room and across his bed. At the bottom of the window is a brown, leather chair next to a built-in bookshelf and stand. I move between the two and take in the stunning view.

Grayson's warmth is at my back and the slow, sensual touch of his hand moves my hair away from my face and to the side of my shoulder. Tucking me into his arms, he kisses my neck.

"What do you think?"

"It's stunning. Your place is beautiful."

His hand caresses my arm in a gentle, affectionate stroke. "I knew you'd like this too."

"The way you keep saying that, it seems you already know me so well."

Under his breath, a chuckle escapes. "You have an appreciation for the rare and beautiful. It's a quality we both share."

I turn in his arms and catch a glimpse of his smile. "You've outdone yourself tonight. The amazing dinner, show, now this. If I didn't know better, I'd say you're trying to seduce me, Mr. Cole."

"And if I am?"

His intense stare stirs my growing affection for him. My head lowers as my confused emotions churn in my belly. I want to trust him, but when the last man you loved tore your heart out, it's difficult to take the leap.

Grayson's fingers touch my chin and raises my gaze to meet his. "You're not over the breakup, are you?"

"We were together for two years. He betrayed me and left as though I never meant anything to him."

Staring into my eyes, I see a shift in Grayson's. A new emotion he hasn't shown before. "When someone breaks your heart, Emma, you have two choices; let it weaken you or let it strengthen you. The choice is yours."

A stray tear falls down my cheek and Grayson's thumb wipes it away. Another follows as the pain of Derrick's betrayal rises to the surface.

"I'm so sorry, I can't believe I'm crying."

Great! An incredibly amazing guy goes above and beyond to impress you and you cry over your ex right in front of him! Is this seriously happening right now?

"How about a drink?"

I nod in silence, keeping my bubbling tears at bay.

As Grayson leaves the room, I walk to his bed and collapse onto it, utterly embarrassed and struggling to compose myself. Looking up, I see the door to his bathroom and go into it, hoping to clean up my tear stained face. My jaw drops when I walk in and look to the left. There's a large, clawfoot bathtub that faces a full glass window with the same stunning view as his bedroom. To the right is an oval, chiseled marble sink elevated from the counter, a fancy toilet, and a walk-in shower.

Moving to the sink, I grab two tissues from the box and begin cleaning the trail of mascara.

Grayson comes in and stops in the door frame, watching me as I dab tissues under my eyes.

I look at him through the mirror and even though I think I look like I got in a fight with a clown, his expression is oddly content, satisfied even.

Nervous with the way he's looking at me, I turn my gaze to the bathtub. "It's amazing. I think we should be roommates just so I can use it."

"Would you like to?"

My gaze shifts to him. "Now?"

The corner of his mouth curves. "Yes, now. I'll draw a bath for you."

Coming into the bathroom, he hands me a short glass with clear, fizzy liquid.

"What is it?"

Approaching the bath, he turns the knobs, adjusting them to the right temperature. "Ice 101 and Sprite."

"Thank you." I gulp enthusiastically as I watch him, astonished that he'd do this for me. "I can't believe you're letting me use your bathtub."

He leans against the tub as the water spills into it. "Will you enjoy it?"

I think every woman has a fantasy of soaking in a fancy tub like this and the view in front of it is an added piece of paradise. How could I not enjoy it? "Yes. Of course."

"That's what matters."

Grayson moves to a standing cabinet by the door

and pulls out a gray, fluffy towel. Approaching me, he takes my empty glass and sets both the glass and towel on the sink counter.

"Close your eyes," he instructs, his voice smooth and commanding.

I do and soon feel the embrace of his hands on my thighs, gradually lifting my dress. Slowly, he raises it until the cool air touches my naked skin. I nibble my lip, fidgety now that he's stopped touching me.

"You're as gorgeous as I imagined."

The sound of him moving behind me builds my anticipation. Slowly his hands wrap around my waist, and I'm pulled to his bare chest. With a soft sweep of his hand, my hair is brushed away from my shoulder. Feathered kisses are given to my neck and down to my collarbone.

My nipples harden and heat rises in my core. Grayson's affectionate touch lowers to my hips and I feel the warmth of his body coming closer to my legs. I glance down to see him untying one of my heels. Raising his gaze to mine, I see a hunger in his eyes that stirs my arousal to a ravenous need.

"I didn't say open your eyes."

I giggle and close them, grinning like a fool. A kiss is pressed to my inner thigh before he grasps my foot and lifts it out of my high heel. The damp trail of his tongue lingers on my other thigh before he lifts my foot out of the other high heel.

I'm soaking wet for him, convulsing with a desperate need, stronger than any I've felt before.

"Grayson," his name escapes my parted lips.

His lips meet mine and mold them into a passionate kiss. My hair is fisted in his hand as he caresses my cheek and holds me close to him. When his lips part, I let out a surprised breath as I'm lifted into his arms.

Heated water, soft as silk, touches my skin and swallows my bare body up to my breasts. I hear the sound of the knobs being turned off. A gentle stroke of Grayson's hand brushes my hair away from my face.

"Open your eyes, Princess."

The view is magnificent and so much more stunning when you're soaking in a beautiful bathtub. My edginess settles and I turn to admire him. He's shirtless, baring hard, muscled arms, chest, and abs. My arousal intensifies at the sight of him and the two tattoos I see. The one on his forearm snakes up and across his bicep, over his shoulder, in dark tribal designs and ends with birds in flight. On his ribs is dark cursive scripture that disappears into the waistline of his pants.

I glance at his zipper and my cheeks flush. Eyeing me steadily he reaches for his pants, unzips them and lets them hang open.

"Want me in the bath with you?"

Silently I nod, unable to tear my gaze from his heated one. I admire the show as he removes his shoes, socks, then pants. My eyes widen at the hardened bulge barely hidden by his black briefs. With his thumbs in the waistband, he pulls them down, releasing his growing erection.

His cock is perfect, thick, and my body is responding from the sight of it. I gnaw my lip between my teeth as my arousal heats between my legs. His erection grows as I stare at him. Looking down at me, his smile is wicked. Surely, he knows what he incites with that massive tool of his. I'm eager for him to join me and move forward, making room.

Stepping in, he settles behind me and pulls me to him. His erection slides between my cheeks and I let out an aroused whimper. For the first time, Grayson's hands settle on my breasts, filling his palms as he thumbs over my nipples. His tongue meets my ear and he pulls the lobe between his teeth, raising goose bumps along my skin.

"I want you in my bed, bare, and begging for me, Emma, but I don't think this is the right night for it. Not when you're still hurting the way you are."

My body and my heart are raging a war. I've never wanted a man so much in my life, but moving forward intimately with Grayson opens my heart up to the worst possible heartbreak because I can see a future with Grayson far better than anything I saw with Derrick.

His breath is warm on my ear as his fingers graze along my stomach. "Tonight, let me help you forget that pain."

My breath catches when his finger slides into me. I let out a moan when a second digit joins the other. My back naturally arches as his strokes deepen. My hair is bunched in his fist and tugged, adding to my pleasure.

"That's it, Emma. Let go for me." His tongue touches my neck first, followed by erotic bites and sucking along my collarbone and shoulder.

My moans echo against the walls as his thumb presses against my clit and his pace steadies into a rhythm. My body quivers as my orgasm builds and with one strong pulse, my release frees my body.

Still trembling in his arms, his kisses soften and he leans back, resting me against his chest.

I'm lost in my own euphoria, satisfied and selfishly enjoying it. As I adjust my position, I feel him rock hard against me. I move over him and a low grumble escapes his lips.

"Emma, I'm barely restraining myself from fucking your tight little hole. Keep wiggling like that and I'll bend you over this tub."

I giggle and slowly raise myself out of the bathtub, pulling the plug as I stand. Grayson watches me with interest. I step out and glancing at him over my shoulder, I catch him admiring my curves. Taking the towel from the sink, I stand in front of him and dry off, lingering at my breasts. Dropping the towel to my feet, I curl my finger for him to get out.

As he stands, his erection stretches. My tongue runs along my bottom lip. The sight of him renews the heat between my legs. I want him, and I want him bad. He steps out and I lower to my knees, resting on the towel.

Realizing my plan brings a wicked smile to Grayson's face and that smile encourages me further. As he steps closer, he affectionately caresses my cheek.

Taking the length of him in my hand surprises me. His girth is wider than it looks. I raise my other hand, massaging him below as I take him into my mouth. Tipping his head back, he groans as I push him to the back of my throat. His fist tightens on my hair and his hips thrust in rhythm with my sucking.

My pace is steady, but my mouth is already sore from the size of him. Any longer and I feel like I'll have lock-jaw. Sucking Grayson off is like running a freaking marathon. I'm exhausted. Relief fills me when he winds my hair around his hand and firms his grip. I feel him expand in my mouth then an explosion of hot cum shoots down my throat.

Grayson looks down at me with heavy lids. Beneath them, his eyes are glossed over and his expression is a mixture of satisfaction and affection.

The touch of his hand caresses along my jaw. With two fingers beneath my chin, he applies gentle pressure and I raise to my feet.

His gaze is steady on mine. There's emotion in his eyes, but he doesn't share it. Instead, he expresses it in his kiss. The passion he releases leaves my head spinning.

"Stay with me tonight?"

My mouth quirks. "I thought I was."

Grayson grins, then turns me and smacks my ass. "Get in my bed, Emma. The night is still young."

CHAPTER 9

GRAYSON

HE EROTIC BOOK IN MY hand is barely distracting me from the stunning woman lying in my bed. Her dark, wavy hair is cascading over the pillow and the sheet barely covers her. From my chair, I have a perfect view of the curve of her back, narrow waist, and luscious ass. She groans as she moves and my cock hardens from the sound. She's learned I have certain tastes in the bedroom. I'd never belittle or hurt a woman, but I do like some kink. No doubt she's a little sore from the vibrator I used. If the sounds of her moans and the two orgasms meant anything, I'd say she liked it very much. My lips curve from the memory of her face when I brought it out and then again when she reached her first climax.

Reaching down, I adjust my semi into a more comfortable position. Little does Emma know how often she gives me a hard on. It's like I'm a fucking teenager again with an uncontrollable snake in my pants that becomes alert and ready anytime it gets a whiff of her pussy.

What's even more confusing is what I'm feeling for her. I've never been patient with sex. I've seduced, got what I wanted, and moved on. It's been this way for years. No woman has ever mattered enough that I wanted to be patient, careful, and even considerate of her emotions. But Emma's inside my head, an itch I can't satisfy until I have her, all of her. With her, I want to take the seduction slowly. I'm enjoying it. She appreciates everything I do, and I find myself upping the ante just to win her affections.

Fear isn't something a man likes to admit to others, let alone to himself, but I feel it. It's there. I'm afraid I'll hurt her. I want her to trust me because if she gives me her trust, I'll have her. But, then what? She'll be another conquest and I'll what, get bored like I always do, lose interest? Or will it be me that burns? If I let her in, I'll have to change. I'll have to give her the trust I know she'll want from me. Am I even capable of giving it, of loving someone?

She stirs in her sleep and I watch her. Emma has no idea she's the first woman to have stayed the night with me. It's probably why I'm up at two a.m. reading because I can't sleep. Not with her lying next to me, smelling like sex and jasmine, and breathing so peacefully it pains me to look at her.

"Grayson," her voice is a sleepy whisper.

I continue watching her move. The sheet falls from her breasts as she sits up and turns to face me. The question in her eyes kills me. She's concerned why I'm not in bed with her. Stepping from the bed, she approaches. Her dark, little patch above her pink lips annihilates my remaining control over my cock.

"Can't sleep?" she asks, her voice so sweet it breaks me.

I extend my arm and she slides onto my lap and lies against my chest, like we've been doing this for years. The scent of jasmine fills my nostrils and I lean against her hair, breathing her in. The touch of my hand caressing her back releases a pleasured moan from her lips. Lips that can easily bring me to my knees, if I'm not careful.

"Sorry to wake you. I read when I can't sleep."

Laying her head on my shoulder, she looks at my book. "What are you reading?"

"Undo This Night."

"Will you read it to me?"

The corner of my mouth raises. "You want me to read it out loud to you?"

She giggles and the sound widens my smile.

"Yes."

This is unexpected, but I like it. She continues to surprise me. I can never predict what Emma will do, and it's something I adore about her. She keeps me on top of my game.

"From the beginning or where I'm at?"

"Where you're at."

My attention returns to the book. "I raise Tiffany's ass in the air and slap it once, twice then spread her cheeks.

Reaching for the condom I tossed on the bed, I sheath it over my cock, then rub against her pink, tiny hole. Looking over her shoulder at me tells me she wants me to fuck her hard. It's been two weeks since I've seen her and by the needy look in her eyes, she knows I won't be gentle."

Emma's hand reaches into my sweatpants and circles my raging hard on. Each stroke makes it harder to focus on the words.

"I slam into her tight pussy and latch onto her hips, using them as leverage to fuck the moans right out of her mouth."

Emma pushes the book out of her way and straddles me with her knees tucked into the cushion of my chair. Her mouth slams down on mine and I toss the book to who-fucking-cares where. Lifting her from the chair, I wrap her legs around me and pull her ass up against my aching erection and move her over it.

"Grayson, I want you. I want to feel you inside of me."

"No other men, Emma. If you're with me, you're with *only* me."

"I don't want anyone else."

Laying her on the bed, she watches as I remove my sweatpants. My cock is at attention and her eyes go right to it. She moistens her bottom lip and it jumps at the sight of it. The last time that tongue touched my dick, she stole a chunk of my heart. Wicked little thing she is.

"Let me get a condom." I move toward the dresser and she extends her legs, trapping me between them.

"Don't need one. I'm on the pill."

My chest tightens. Sex without a condom is something I *don't* do. Fuck me, she's got me between a rock and a soft, little pussy I'm dying to feel. I turn to her and crawl above her on the bed. "Just this once. I want to feel you come all over my cock."

Her gray eyes are locked on mine and her mouth tilts into a lascivious grin. I close the space between us and kiss her. Spreading her legs, my dick slides across her slick pussy. She's already soaking wet for me. I raise my hips and plunge into her.

Cock-melting heat surrounds me, she's so tight I barely have to move to get the friction I need. Pushing in further, she lets out a whimper.

"Am I hurting you?"

"No, you feel incredible."

"Emma, I want to give you slow and sensual, but I don't think I can. I want to fuck you until you're calling out my name."

"Please, fuck me," she begs.

Her needy plea puts me into action. One hand takes hold of her neck and the other tucks under her leg, raising it as I thrust into her hard. Every time I pull out and slam into her, I feel the blood racing to my groin. The familiar tingle is at my back; she's spewing cuss words and calling out my name. Another thrust and her orgasm pours over me and it feels perfect.

My jaw clenches and I release into her. It's a high I've never had and the moment it happens, I know I'm ruined. There's no way I can go back to a condom with her.

Lying on the bed, she's sprawled out across my body in a deep sleep with her head tucked into my neck. My fingers are combing through her hair and I'm watching the ceiling, replaying different scenarios in my head. Every single one ends with the same fear— one of us getting hurt.

CHAPTER 10

EMMA

*W*HEN I WAKE, IT TAKES me a moment to realize where I am and that Grayson is gone. I look around for my dress, heels, phone, everything. I don't even know what time it is. Glancing around, I find a clock on his nightstand. It's six after eight. I'm supposed to be at work already. I hurry and dress, then walk into Grayson's kitchen. He's nowhere around. I shoot off a text to him.

Where are you?

Work.

Why didn't you wake me up?

You looked too peaceful to wake up.

But now I'm late for work!

I'm your Boss. You can make it up to me.

Grayson!

Take your time. See you when you get here.

How do I get home??

The keys are on the counter.

I look on the counter and sure enough, there's a set of keys. To what, I don't know. I grab them and take the elevator down to the parking garage. I hit the key fob and his silver sports car honks. *You're fucking kidding me.*

I've been given keys to his fancy-ass sports car. Yeah, like I need to wreck this and owe him undoubtedly seventy grand or more. Pulling out my phone, I call a cab.

When the cab arrives at my apartment, I pay him, then hurry up the stairs, rush through a shower, find something cute to wear, put my hair into a long ponytail, grab my keys, and leave for work. On the way to work, I get breakfast and coffee then rush up to our floor. Thankfully, no one sees me and I slip into my office unnoticed.

Moments later, the door swings open and Claire stands there, an inquisitive look on her face. *I'm so busted.*

"Why are you so late? And why did Grayson come in a cab this morning? I saw him getting out when I pulled into the parking garage. And where's your rose?"

I glance at my desk, equally surprised as her. "I don't know."

"Ok, what happened last night?"

I spin my chair to face her and cross my legs. After two days of no underwear in the office, it's odd to feel them now. "He took me to dinner, the Dirty Dancing show, then I stayed the night at his house." I speed release the last few words as my cheeks grow warm.

Her surprise is apparent by her parted lips and wide eyes. "And? Did you have sex?"

I nod, tight-lipped.

"Was it good?"

"Sooo good. Multiple O's good."

"This is so juicy. Like romance book juicy. You're having an office affair with your Boss!"

"Yes," I giggle. "I'm totally banging my hot Boss."

My phone rings and my attention whips to it. Grayson's office line blinks on the screen. My nerves combust as I reach for it. "Yes?"

"I need you in here, Princess." Just the sound of his voice brings heat between my legs and a tingle in my stomach.

"On my way."

I hang up and look to Claire. "I'm being summoned."

"This conversation is *definitely* not finished. Let's have lunch together."

"You got it. See ya in a while."

We both walk out of my office and I head to Grayson's. The windows are shaded white and I smile at the memory of what happened the last two times his office windows were shaded. I open the door and walk in. On the edge of the desk is one single white rose. My heart skips a beat. He's surprised me again.

I lift the rose and inhale its sweet fragrance. "For me?"

BETTY SHREFFLER

Grayson leans back in his chair and admires me and my outfit. "I'll excuse that silly question because you look too damn good for me to waste time being upset. Of course, it's for you."

Moving closer to his chair, I raise my leg and lean my ass and heel against his desk. "Thank you. I love them. I had an amazing time last night too."

Grayson's jaw pinches tight and I wonder what the cause is. His gaze falls to my bent leg and his hand stretches out, caressing my thigh. "I'd like you to stay again."

My body awakens with need, tingling with desire at the simple touch of his hand. "What about my place? I'd love for you to come over. I'd even dust off my pans and make you something."

Grayson's hand reaches farther up my skirt and grazes the front of my panties. My breath quickens and my grip on the rose tightens. "You want to cook for me?"

I lose my breath at the warmth of his caress. Closing my eyes, I give into the sensation drifting through my body. "Yes."

He stands, removing his touch. My eyes shoot open, only to close as his lips contact mine. His kiss is slow, sensual, affectionate even. It takes me by surprise.

Grayson steps closer, erasing the space between us. Sliding me off the desk, he pulls me flush against him. One hand takes hold of my ass as the other brushes my cheek, then holds the nape of my neck. His kiss deepens and I feel that colossal pole harden.

The door to his office suddenly opens and I jolt out of his arms as he pulls away from our kiss. I turn to see a tall, handsome man with brown, peppered hair in a gray suit look at us both, then smirk.

"Hi, Son."

Oh my God. Please tell me he didn't see much.

Grayson places his hand on my back. "Emma, this is my father, Arnold Cole."

Mr. Cole nods pleasantly. "Emma, it's a pleasure."

My nerves splinter, tingling throughout my body. I have no doubt my face is bright red. "Likewise," I manage to say.

"Emma, I need to speak with my father alone. I'll come by your office later."

Grayson rubs my back as I step away, giving me a bit of reassurance. I smile as I walk past Mr. Cole. As soon as I'm out of the office, I release the breath I didn't realize I was holding.

—GRAYSON—

"Don't fucking look at her like that," I snarl.

Arnold's attention returns to me now that Emma has left my office. He adjusts his suit jacket and smirks like the asshole he is.

"Look at her like what?"

"Like she's a pretty piece of ass."

"From the looks of what I walked in on, I'd say that's precisely what she is."

Keeping my anger restrained, I adjust my wrist watch and clear my throat. "Tell me you have a good reason for being in my office."

"Coming to see my favorite son isn't enough of a reason?" His attempt to fake insult is pathetic.

"I'm your *only* son."

Arnold shrugs. "That I know of."

I roll my eyes. "Reason…for being here?"

"I thought we'd have lunch and go over business."

"Still hoping to sway my vote on the board?"

He scoffs. "Never should have given you those shares."

A grin lifts the corner of my mouth. "Best decision you made and you know it. I keep you and the board of directors honest."

Arnold walks toward my window and looks out at the view. "Yes, my righteous son. So honest and caring." He turns to face me, his expression cocky. "How is Liza, Marie or was it, Michelle? Whatever flavor of the month she was?"

I chuckle at his jab. "Her name was Madison and that was over two months ago."

Tucking his hands into his pockets, he stands proud, with his usual superiority. "And this Emma woman, what is she to you?"

My jaw tightens. "Emma is not up for discussion."

He tilts his head and frowns. "Don't tell me you've developed feelings for this woman."

"Are you getting hard of hearing in your old age?"

Arnold waves his hand. "Old, please. If I was old, I wouldn't have fucked a woman in her twenties two nights ago."

"Yeah, that Viagra works wonders."

"You little shit."

He laughs and I do too.

"Are we going to have lunch or are you going to make your *old* man starve?"

When we step out of the office, I see Emma collecting her mail from the boxes in the lobby. Thankfully, Arnold's too busy checking out every female in my office to notice her. Her eyes catch mine and that sweet, seductive smile of hers bewitches me. Thoughts of what I want to do to her while pulling on that lengthy ponytail flash through my mind.

Arnold catches the direction of my gaze and I cut our eye contact. The last thing I want is for him to take an interest in what she means to me.

CHAPTER 11

EMMA

*A*FTER LUNCH, I GO INTO speed reading mode. I'm just about finished with the second book I want to send to Grayson and need to find one more good one to meet my deadline of three this week. Looks like it's going to be a late night at the office. Hopefully, he won't be disappointed if it takes until Monday to get him the third book. It's such an awkward position to be in; wanting to satisfy your Boss, but also hoping it won't be long until he's satisfying me with another orgasm.

My door is open and I hear Grayson's voice in the lobby when he returns from his lunch. There's something so seductive about that man's voice. Just the sound of it sends a bolt of arousal straight to my vagina.

The sound of his feet nears my office, then I feel his presence looming behind me. I turn and grin, all too happy to see him. "How was your lunch," I ask.

"Too long."

"Did you have a good time with your father?"

With a tight jaw, he frowns. "Fun is a word I would never use when describing anything with him. Do you have my keys?"

His curt responses concern me.

"Oh, yes." I reach into my purse and pull his keys out and hand them to him. "I didn't drive it here though."

"Why?"

"Grayson, you drive a Nissan 370z. I was too afraid of damaging it. It probably costs double what I make in a year."

"It only cost thirty-five thousand, Emma and if I wasn't afraid of you damaging it, you shouldn't have been."

"*Only* thirty-five thousand. I didn't want to risk it."

Grayson turns to leave without saying another word and my stomach knots.

"Grayson."

He turns back to look at me. His thoughts seem a world away.

"I've sent representation for two more authors' manuscripts and will have their packets to you in the next hour. I may not have the third book to you until Monday. Is that okay?"

"It's fine, Emma. You've worked hard on the ones you've sent, but no later than Monday."

He walks out and I'm left feeling confused and a little hurt by his all-business attitude. Not wanting to press the issue, I get back to work sending the emails to the authors and then the packets to Grayson. Thirty minutes later, I open a new manuscript Lisa sent me and dive in. Twenty minutes later, I close that manuscript, respond to Lisa that I've rejected it and move onto the next. This happens three more times and I'm becoming concerned I might not meet Grayson's deadline. I open the fifth manuscript and thankfully this one sucks me in enough I want to keep reading.

The bright sun outside my office window has moved to the other side of the building and the sky is now a dark gray, hinting at a rain shower. When I hear the taps on the window, my attention is pulled away from the computer. I stand and stretch my legs and glance out at the thunderstorm rolling across the sky. My thoughts go to Grayson and I wonder if something happened during his lunch that upset him. Glancing at the clock, I see it's already past my time off. I'm not surprised.

Looking into the lobby, I see everyone's offices are blacked out with doors closed except Grayson's. His windows are clear and he's steadily typing away at his computer, clearly focused on work.

I enter and he slowly stops typing, then looks to me. His eyes narrow a bit as if I'm disrupting him. "Yes, Emma?"

"Are you okay? You seemed upset earlier."

"I'm fine. You should head home. It's late and the weather is going to get worse."

Again, he's curt with me and it stings. I turn to leave, but I don't want to go feeling this way. "What about dinner? Would you like to come over tonight?"

Grayson raises his attention to me. "Thank you, but not tonight."

Tears irritate my eyes and I leave his office with a lump in my throat and a ball of emotion in my gut.

AT HOME, I'VE CHANGED INTO lounge pants, a fitted t-shirt, and slippers and nestled into my blue, comfy couch with my tablet. I'm ready to finish the manuscript I started earlier. Several pages in and I'm gnawing on my lip as the tantalizing words bring heat between my legs. A knock on my door yanks my thoughts from the story. I grumble, not in the mood to entertain anyone after Grayson's rejection and weird attitude this afternoon.

Opening the door, Grayson stands there in jeans and a jacket, his hair a wet and sexy mess, a bag of food in his hand.

"Can I come in?"

I open the door wider and he steps in, sets the food down and shakes off his jacket and raindrops. He hangs his jacket in my closet, then grabs the bag of food. "I picked us up something, where would you like me to put it?"

I point to the counter in the kitchen. I'm thrilled to see him, but a bit confused. "I'm surprised to see you."

He quietly sets the food down then takes the few steps over to me. "I needed to see you." Lifting me up, he spreads my legs around his waist and holds my ass tight against him. "Where's your bedroom?"

Already feeling wet and needy from the sex scene in the book, I giggle and point toward the hall. Maybe I should be turning him down and demand an explanation for his behavior earlier, but you know what, a woman has needs too, and in this moment, I want the release.

He nips and sucks at my neck, then consumes my mouth with his fiery and eager kiss. "I want to bury myself in you and forget this day."

His voice is gruff, filled with sexual need. I'm tossed onto my bed and looking up, I see his eyes have glossed over. The desire is there and my body responds, ready and willing to be taken by him.

My slippers drop to the floor as he quickly removes my pants and underwear. Next, my t-shirt is thrown through the air followed by him removing his sweater and revealing his perfectly toned torso. The rest of his clothes disappear as quickly as mine.

His weight lowers the bed as he crawls above me. Placing his hands on my knees, he spreads my legs and the moment his tongue touches my clit, I know he means business. He tongue-fucks the shit out of me and I grab his hair and uncontrollably bounce my hips toward his face, riding my high.

As soon as the trembling from my orgasm fades, he raises himself, grabs my legs, and flips me over. Raising my ass to him, he spreads my legs, then fills me to the brim.

A low moan escapes his lips before he holds my hips steady and pounds into me. I fist my comforter and moan so loud I have to shove my face into the pillow so I don't scare my neighbors.

"Fuuuck, Emma. You feel so good."

His hand latches onto my shoulder and he fucks me harder. The sound of moans, grunts and skin slapping skin echoes in my ears. He feels incredible. I don't want it to end, but my own body is a greedy bitch and I slam back into him, eager for another orgasm.

As I pour over him, I feel his dick pulse, then release into me. The tight grip on my shoulder relaxes as he pulls out. He leans over me, bites my ear and pulls it between his teeth. Goosebumps raise over my skin as his hands rub down my arms. "Liked that, didn't you?"

"Yes."

Grayson leans up on his knees and raises me with him, holding me against his chest as his hands massage my breasts. His hot breath warms my ear. "Next time, I want it in your ass, Princess. Would you like that?"

I let out a whimper as he thumbs my sensitive nipples. "Yes."

His head is buried in my hair and he's holding me tight against him. "What else would you let me do?"

I chuckle. "Nothing, until you feed me, Grayson Cole. I did see the restaurant name on that bag you brought in."

Grayson laughs into my ear. "Maybe I'm not ready to let you out of this bed."

"Fine, but I want to know what upset you this afternoon."

Dropping his arms, he steps off the bed and gathers his clothes. His jaw is locked and he looks irritated.

"Grayson, what's wrong?"

He raises his jeans over his hips, then zips them. "I came to see you to forget about today, not to be badgered about it."

Ouch! "Ok, sorry I asked. I was worried about you." Feeling upset, I gather my own clothes and head out of the room toward my bathroom.

"Emma." His voice stills my footsteps.

I turn to look at him, holding my clothes to my chest, covering myself. "*Grayson?*"

"You're mad?"

"Yes. You've been acting like a dick all afternoon."

Pulling the sweater over his body, he frowns. "Then why'd you let me fuck you?"

I'm taken aback by the brashness. "Because."

"Why?"

"Because I have feelings for you and I wanted to be with you!"

"You shouldn't have feelings for me."

I switch my footing as irritation builds in my chest. "Ok, I'm not having this conversation while standing here naked. I'm getting dressed, putting food in my belly and then afterward you can rattle off insanity."

His lips curve into a humored smile. "All right, get dressed. I'll get the food ready."

When I come out of my bathroom, Grayson has the plates filled and placed at my small, round dining table.

As I approach, he grabs me and pulls me into his arms. His eyes soften as he stares down at me. "I'm sorry I acted like a dick today. My father and I don't always see eye to eye on things and he knows what buttons to push to upset me. He can be a real asshole when he wants something his way."

The fact that Grayson is opening up to me brings me an immense amount of relief and joy. I wrap my arms around his neck, running my fingers through his hair. Closing his eyes for a moment, he gives into the sensation. Tilting his head, he kisses my arm, then opens his eyes and looks at me with affection in his eyes.

"What did your father say to upset you?"

His hand raises and brushes my hair away from my face before caressing my cheek. I lean into his warm touch. "It's not something I want to discuss. I'd rather enjoy this night with you."

"I understand and I mean that when I say it. My own mother and I are prone to arguments particularly about my job, marriage, and when I'm going to have children. She wants grandchildren so bad, she gave

Derrick and me an ovulation kit last Christmas. That *did not* go over well. Now that I think back on it, I can see how bad that was for our relationship."

Grayson chuckles. "That's a little crazy. You know that, right?"

I laugh. "Yes. I love her, but she is crazy."

His brows pinch inward in thought. "You know it's twice now you've brought up your ex when we're together?"

My eyes widen. He's right, I have. "I'm sorry. Does it bother you?"

"Yes. I don't like imagining any other man being with you."

His words enchant me. A smile swells my cheeks. "It makes you jealous?"

"Not jealous. I don't want any other man to touch you like I do."

"Feeling possessive of me?"

"I am. I want to be the only one to have this." Reaching down, he caresses between my legs.

My breath catches as my body heats up. "I want you to be the only one to have it."

Grayson's eyes search mine. "Only say it if you mean it, Emma."

"I do."

Grayson releases me, and turns me toward the table, squeezing my ass before he steps to the other side. "Hurry and eat, Princess. I want to have you again after dinner."

I'm a little buzzed with anticipation as I sit down to

eat. Grayson walks over to the counter and opens the bottle of wine he set out. Filling two glasses, he brings them to the table.

"Thank you," I say as he hands me a glass.

He winks and takes a seat across from me. "I had a look at both of the manuscripts you sent me today. I've extended a contract for *Savage Romance* and as long as the writer of *Swept Away* accepts your offer of representation, I'll extend a contract for that one as well. You make my job easy. I'm beginning to feel that anything you send me is contract worthy."

I take a bite of the lamb Grayson reheated and it's still delicious, but not as satisfying as his words. "That means a lot to me."

"You definitely have a skill for discovering talent."

"Better than Rachel?"

Grayson swallows his bite and the corner of his mouth lifts. "Yes, Emma. Better than Rachel. She gets under your skin, doesn't she?"

"She's a bitch."

"Not to me."

My eyes narrow and Grayson laughs before taking another bite.

"Of course she's not to you. She wants to ride that eight-inch pole of yours."

Grayson shakes his head. "Not going to happen, Emma."

"I know, but I disliked her before that. She's always been a bitch."

"Tell me how you truly feel."

I laugh and Grayson does too.

"Do you still need the third book by Monday? I'm about halfway through one now and if it continues to be as good as it is so far, I'll be sending it to you."

"Depends."

My brows turn in. "On what?"

"How busy I keep you this weekend." His smile is mischievous.

I nibble my lip and rub my thighs together.

Grayson's gaze lingers on me and his eyes give away his desire. "Emma, are you getting wet thinking about my dick inside you?"

I cross my legs and the pressure increases my arousal. "Yes," I respond bashfully.

Grayson clicks his tongue. "Have you had enough to eat?"

"I have." I move the nearly empty plate away as Grayson stands from the table. Coming to my side, he takes my hand, raising me from the chair.

Taking a step closer, he kisses me and the need I feel between my legs starts to throb. His arm wraps around my back, holding me close as his other hand works my pants off my hips.

NEXT TO ME, GRAYSON IS in a deep sleep, comfortably resting in my bed. My expectation of him being a beast in the bedroom has been surpassed. I'm half tempted to nickname his penis Zeus the almighty. What makes it even better was the caressing and cuddling I received before he fell asleep. I'm completely falling for him and it's been what—a week? This is insane!

Part of me feels I need to pull back to protect my heart, but I'm afraid if I do I might lose him. Sometimes I feel like I'm holding onto him by a thread —at any minute he'll decide he's not interested in me any longer and the truth is, that would crush me.

I turn to my side and watch him sleep. He's so handsome it's astonishing. I want to bottle up his sexy and sell it in a perfume. I'd be rich. Reaching out, I caress his face. I wish he felt comfortable sharing with me what it was his father said to upset him. He's still so closed off and it's frustrating. It's as if he's keeping me at arm's length.

One of his eyes opens, then the other. He reaches out an arm, and wrapping it around me, he pulls me against him. "I fell asleep?"

I press my lips to his and kiss him. "You did."

"You make me feel relaxed." The affectionate strokes of his fingers through my hair send a pleasurable sensation through my entire body.

"Great sex does that to you."

He chuckles. "It's more than your sweet pussy." His hand leaves my hair and his finger swipes across my lip making me tingle with need. Good grief, I'm a glutton for his touch.

"I was hoping you felt that way."

Wrapping an arm around me, he holds me against him and turns his body, so I'm lying on top of him. Raising his head, he kisses me, slow and passionate. His hands take hold of my ass and press me into his erection. I rock my hips, sliding over him, back and forth.

"Emma, turn around and ride me." His words are barely more than a whisper, yet his voice holds its usual air of confidence.

I'm eager to please and try this position with him. I adjust my leg and turn. Taking him in my hand, I slide him in. One hand rubs along my back, then takes hold of my hip while the other grabs my hair and winds it around his fist.

I rock my hips, finding the best angle before putting feverish momentum into reaching my orgasm. His hand on my hair tightens, tilting my head back and arching my back.

"That's it, Emma. Fuck me with that sweet pussy."

His hand slaps my ass, rubs it tenderly, then slaps again. I moan repeatedly as I near my climax. Grayson's grip on my hair releases, both hands take hold of my hips and add to my momentum, slamming me onto him. He lets out his own moan, then his hips thrust up, filling me entirely as he releases into me.

Completely spent and exhausted, I collapse backward onto his chest. His arms wrap around me, one muscular hand holding me by the neck as he kisses my cheek. "I love the way it feels to have you come all over my cock."

"I love how you make me come...*every single time*."

Grayson smiles into my ear. "How do you feel about me staying the night with you?"

"I was hoping you would." Sliding off him, I nestle into the nook of his shoulder.

He kisses my hair before running his fingers through it. "Do you want to have breakfast together tomorrow morning?"

I smile as his soothing strokes lull me to sleep. "Yes, I do."

CHAPTER 12

GRAYSON

*A*S I WATCH HER SLEEP, I run my fingers over her breast, shoulder, and arm. I can't stop touching her. She's soft as silk and every time I do, her body responds to me like a flame touching oil and I feel it—she's burning herself right into my heart. Shit, that sounded sappy as hell. She's got my head fucked.

When Arnold insisted on discussing her at lunch yesterday, he set me off. He went on one of his rants of how the more beautiful they are, the more deceitful they become. That I need to make sure I don't fall for her pussy, that I need to fuck her and move on. The memories of Danielle flooded my mind and I was ready to end it with Emma before I became even more emotionally involved, but the look on her face when I said no to dinner broke me. I went home, showered and no matter what I did, I couldn't stop thinking of her.

After the mood my father put me in, the only thing I wanted to console me was—her. Everything is better when I'm with her. All the business of life seems to slow down and I'm able to lose myself for as long as she's near.

She stirs and cuddles closer. I settle on my back and wrap my arm around her. I stroke her cheek as she starts to wake. "Morning, Princess."

A smile fills the lower part of her face. Any wider and her puffy cheeks might burst. I know that smile is for me and it gives me an unusual feeling of gratification.

"Grayson."

"Yes, Emma?"

"How old are you?"

I can't help laughing. "It's seven-thirty in the morning and your first thought is how old I am?"

She raises her head, opens her dark, gray eyes and looks at me. Damn, her sleepy, after-sex look is as stunning as when she has her hair styled and high heels on.

"Yes, I want to know."

"I'm thirty-six."

"When is your birthday?"

"Emma."

Her fingers trace circles on my chest, her touch dangerously addictive.

"Tell me, Grayson."

"June fourth."

"Do you want to know mine?"

Brushing my hand over her hair, I kiss her forehead. "I already do. Your birthday is three weeks away."

"How do you…of course, my files."

I chuckle and she lays her head back on my chest.

"I'd like to spend my birthday with you."

Tension constricts my chest. "Emma, we don't know what will be going on in three weeks."

The motion of her finger slows. "You mean with us?"

Damn it, Grayson. Shut this down now.

"I'll look at my schedule. Ok?"

"All right."

She sounds disappointed and I hate it.

"Come on, Princess. Let's get breakfast."

I take her hand and motivate her out of bed with me. She giggles when I lift her off her feet and toss her over my shoulder. The sound lightens my mood. Carrying her into the shower with me, I give her a hard smack on the ass before letting her down.

"Grayson!"

As she rubs her ass, I grin from the red mark I left. Turning the knob, I adjust it to the right temperature then move her under the warm water. I don't know why I have an overwhelming desire to clean her, probably because my horny ass wants to make her dirty again.

As she closes her eyes and places her head under the water, I admire how beautiful she looks. My hands instinctively take hold of her waist and I step forward until the soft lips of her pussy are wrapped around my cock. Leaning in, I kiss her. The passion I feel her give me stiffens my erection. She moves, rubbing herself over it and I'm done for.

I lift her up, wrap her legs around my waist and drive into her wet folds. Her moans fuel my appetite. Tightening my grip on her thigh and back, I thrust my hips hard, over and over, until she's crying out my name and the heat of her orgasm surrounds me.

"I can't get enough of you, Emma."

"Then don't." Her wet lips touch mine and the passion I feel in her kiss burns right through me. I explode into her while holding her lips hostage.

Damn it, what is she doing to me?

Easing out of her, I let her down and grab the yellow bottle of shampoo. Pouring some in my hand, I smooth it over her hair then turn her back to me so I can get to work. Her quiet moans of pleasure please me. Turning her back to the water, I rinse her hair before lathering her body with her jasmine body wash. This stuff right here is how she stays so soft—it's silk in a bottle.

After ensuring every part of her is clean, she takes the spongy thing from my hand and goes to put soap on it for me.

"No, Princess. We're not making my junk smell like jasmine."

She laughs and it widens my smile.

As I shampoo my hair and rinse off, she steps out of the shower, humming, sounding incredibly happy. A knot forms in my chest.

This is getting to be too much, too fast. She's falling for you, you asshole.

I start to doubt my plans for breakfast and to have her in my bed the whole weekend. Maybe it's time to put space between us.

"I'm coming!"

I hear her shout from outside the bathroom. The sound of it surprises me, breaking me from my thoughts. I didn't even hear a knock or doorbell. I quickly grab the towel outside the shower and begin drying myself, as she walks past the bathroom, already dressed.

Entering her room, I find my clothes quickly. I hear her squeal with joy and my jaw tightens. It better not be another man.

Entering her living room, I try to see who's standing on the other side of her door. "Emma, who is it?" My tone demanding.

Megan burst through the door carrying a tiny, black, curly-haired puppy. "It's a miniature poodle," she says to Emma.

Relief fills my chest and I laugh as Emma and Megan both lose their sanity over the tiny dog. Closing the door, Emma sits on the floor so the puppy can pounce on her lap. Letting it lick her face, she snuggles it like she already loves it. Seeing her like this gives me odd satisfaction.

"What did you name him?" Emma asks.

"JD," Megan replies.

Emma looks up at Megan. "What's JD stand for?"

"Jack Daniel, the good whiskey."

Emma laughs and I squat down on my knee. JD skips over to me, eager for attention. I pet the cute, little thing and Emma watches me with soft, glossy eyes. Goddamn, I know that look. I nudge the puppy back to her as my phone rings in my back pocket.

"This is Mr. Cole," I answer.

"Mr. Cole, it's Gregory Johnston from Schmidt and Costello, New York. I know this may be short notice, but this week we're having a company-wide meeting and need all branch agents to attend. I apologize you were not notified sooner, there was a discrepancy with your email contact."

"As in someone forgot to send it?"

A low chortle comes through the receiver. "Yes, Mr. Cole, precisely. Can you attend?"

I look to Emma who's questioning eyes are watching me. I swallow the lump in my throat. I suppose my wish has been granted.

"How long will I need to be in New York?"

"Arrive Monday and depart Friday," Gregory replies.

"I can attend. I'll get a flight booked today. Thank you for the courtesy call."

"The details have been emailed to you, Mr. Cole. See you Monday."

I tuck the phone back in my pocket. "Sorry,

Princess, we'll have to postpone breakfast. I need to head back to my place and get a flight booked to leave for New York on Monday."

"Ok, that's fine. Megs and I can go out instead. How long will you be gone?" I know she's hiding her disappointment, I can hear it in her tone. The sound of it bothers me too much.

Standing, she comes to me. I pull her into my arms and run my thumb along her jaw, wanting to feel her one last time before I go. "I'll be gone all week. Can you take care of things at the office for me while I'm gone?"

"Of course." She gives me a forced smile and I kiss her cheek, ready to leave before this gets any more difficult.

"I'll call you," I say as I thumb her pouty lip.

"Ok."

Letting her out of my arms, I grab my jacket from the closet before heading out.

—EMMA—

MEGAN'S EYES FOLLOW GRAYSON'S BACK as he leaves. After the door closes, her gaze returns to me. "Did he stay the night?"

I nod as I pick JD up from the floor and walk to the couch. "He did."

Megs joins me. "So, are you two together?"

A frown forms on my face. "Honestly, I don't know what we are. He's incredibly hard to read. I feel like he's keeping me at arm's length and not letting himself get too close. Granted it's only been a week."

"Just be careful. He might be using you for sex. I don't want to see you invest a lot of feelings and get hurt."

I lower my head and pet JD, not wanting to admit it's too late.

"You already have feelings, don't you?"

"How could I not? We've been sleeping together, and Megan, he's freaking huge!"

JD bounces out of my arms and scurries over to Megan to snuggle. Megan laughs as she places her hand over JD's back.

"Lucky bitch. I bet he's good in bed too."

"So good!"

"Of course he is. Maybe it's a good thing he's going on this trip for the week. It'll give you a chance to get your emotions in check."

Bringing my knees to my chest, I hug them. "I'm gonna miss him."

"Oh man, Em. You got it bad already."

I rub my face, embarrassed. "Jeez, oh man. I do. Let's go get breakfast. I need food and girl-time to snap out of the sulking mood I'm dangling on the edge of."

Lifting JD in her arms, she stands from the couch.

"Yes, let's go. I haven't had any food yet, I was too excited to bring JD over."

"You know he's adorable, right? You're gonna have to stop me from trying to steal him."

"I might be willing to arrange dual custody," she says with a wink.

CHAPTER 13

I SPENT THE REST OF the weekend hoping I'd see Grayson again, but he didn't call on Sunday. Monday morning there's no rose and disappointment slams into my gut. I turn on the computer and check my emails. There's an all-staff email from Grayson letting us know he had to take a business trip to New York this week and that he left me in charge. The fact that he left me with that responsibility gives me a bit of pride, but in all honesty, I was the best choice. I'm the most experienced and the highest ranking agent, besides Rachel.

I barely get through my never-ending list of emails when I hear heels smack across the floor. I turn to see Rachel huffing and puffing and ready to blow down my office. "Guess you learned sex gets you what you want after all."

Rolling my eyes, I turn back to my computer. "What are you chirping about?"

"Grayson made you Boss for the week. You and I both know it's because you're sucking his dick every morning."

Really? This bitch is unreal.

Looking back at her, I lean back in my chair and cross my legs. "He made me the Boss because I'm the most experienced. *We* both know you're jealous about that and I suggest you tone down the accusations of what our Boss is or isn't doing before he gets wind of it and gets pissed off."

Her eyes narrow and she turns and storms out, her heels smacking on the floor with the same fury as when she arrived.

A smile creeps onto my face and lingers when I see Claire heading to my office.

She steps in, her long, red hair in loose curls. She looks adorable in her brown sweater and pink skirt.

"You know I love it when I see Rachel leave your office looking like she wants to slug you, right?"

"I do. I wouldn't be surprised if some day she does."

Closing the door, Claire sits in one of the chairs at the table.

I point to her and move my finger up and down in the air. "I love your outfit."

"Thank you!" She swings her leg over the other and bounces her shoe. My eyes go right to it.

"You got new shoes this weekend!"

"Yes, super cute, aren't they?"

"Yes!"

"Shawn took me shopping. Got two other pairs I can't wait to show you. How was your weekend?"

My mouth twists. "Quiet. I got a lot of reading done."

"You didn't see Grayson at all?"

"We spent Friday together and I know he planned to spend the weekend with me, but then he got the call to go to New York. He left Saturday morning and I haven't heard from him since."

"He must be busy."

"I'm sure he is."

Her head slants as she studies me. "You seem off. What's wrong?"

I let out a breath. "This whole thing with Grayson. I don't know where it's headed. I don't know how he feels or what he wants."

"Em, don't start. You're over-analyzing again."

"Ugh! I know! That's what Megan said too. She told me to make a choice; either enjoy the ride and don't worry about a label of what we are or go all in emotionally and be prepared that it could end in heartbreak or something incredible."

"What choice have you made?"

"Ha! You expected me to make one? I'm gonna go with option C."

Laugh lines form in the corner of her eyes as she giggles. "What's option C?"

I shrug. "I'm not sure yet."

Her laughter brings a smile to my face. The ringing phone cuts through our conversation. It's another client who has a question about something I sent her in the manuscript. Claire quietly excuses herself and I wave goodbye.

—GRAYSON—

ONE FLIGHT, A LAYOVER IN Atlanta, a second flight, and I'm now settled into the Hilton where Schmidt and Costello booked rooms for all of us branch agents. I only know one other agent, Michael Steele, and his text is awaiting my response about drinks at a nearby bar. I shoot a text back.

I'm game as long as the bar serves food.

His response is quick and he confirms they have good burgers and wings. A sports bar isn't my go-to, but it will do.

Entering the bar, I recognize Michael's blond hair and tall stature. He gives a two-finger wave and I join him and another guy who looks like he's been taken right out of a mobster lineup with his slick, black hair and muddy, brown suit.

"Grayson, how are ya, bud?"

"Good, man, ready for a drink after those flights."

Michael points to his company.

"Grayson, this is James Oliver, James this is Grayson Cole."

I outstretch my hand and shake his.

"You're from Florida, right?"

"Yeah, just joined over a week ago."

"Welcome to Schmidt and Costello."

Reaching to the end of the table, I grab a menu. "Thanks. You worked with S&C long?"

"Yeah." James nods. "Six years now."

"Either of you know what this meeting is about? I was called on Saturday to join and haven't received much information."

Michael lowers his beer. "Yeah, I know one of the things they want to discuss. They're opening another branch in Atlanta. They want to know if any of us branch agents have employee recommendations for the new location. They're looking for current, experienced agents to be the new branch agent there."

"You got any good candidates?" James asks.

A weight settles in the pit of my stomach. "Yeah, a couple. Two women that have been working for S&C for five or six years. They're both great employees."

A cute, blonde waitress wearing a cleavage-bearing tank top sashays up to our high-top table. "What can I get you?" she asks with a little more pep than is necessary.

Her eyes linger on me and usually my first thought would be what a fun fuck she'd be while I'm here in New York, but instead, I grimace as the thoughts of Emma flash through my mind. I'd rather it be Emma's pussy I bury myself in. Damn, how I wish she was back at my hotel, naked, spread and waiting for me.

"I'll take a scotch. The best you have. Make it a double."

"You got it, babe. Would you fellas like anything to eat?"

We share our orders and she flashes me a wink before leaving the table.

"I think that hot little number wants a piece of you, Grayson."

"Yeah," I say carelessly as I put the menu back between the condiments.

"You gonna take her back to your hotel?" Michael asks with a wolfish grin.

I shrug and look her direction. She's eyeing me with a fuck-me gaze. She'd probably be an easy screw, in and out of the hotel in an hour, but hell if Emma hasn't gotten in deep. Just the thought of taking this chick back to my hotel room, leaves me with, what the hell is this feeling? Guilt? My jaw is tense when I return my attention back to Michael. "Probably not."

"Got a woman back home?"

I rub the back of my neck. "How long does it take to pour a glass of scotch?"

Michael laughs and takes a swig of his beer. "She must mean something to you if you're turning down that." He points the top of his beer bottle in the direction of the waitress.

"What else is on this week's agenda?" I ask, changing the subject.

Michael and James smirk behind their drinks. *Fuckers.*

"Probably some training and some boring lectures about sales numbers," James responds.

Running my fingers through my hair, I sit back against the back of the bar stool. "This is going be a thrilling week. I can already tell."

CHAPTER 14

GRAYSON

*I*F NOT FOR GREGORY JOHNSTON, the Operations Director, having a sense of humor, this meeting would be excruciating. It's 1:45 on Tuesday, we've finished lunch and gone over the expansion of Schmidt and Costello. We're going around the table and making our suggestions of who on our staff would be a suitable candidate for the new branch agent. I'm next and my body is fucking breaking out in sweat. Last night, I was able to avoid my feelings with cold liquor. Now, there's a festering ball in the pit of my stomach and there's nothing I can do about it. *Unless.*

"Grayson, how about you?" Gregory's voice is like thunder, interrupting my thoughts.

"Rachel Moore," I reply. "Been working with S&C for five years. She has an incredible skill for recognizing talent. This past year she's sold thirty-two manuscripts to publishers. Three made the best sellers list."

Gregory nods, seemingly satisfied. He jots down notes on his pad and switches his attention to James, sitting next to me. Relief loosens the knot in my chest and then it constricts when Gregory looks back at me.

"What about Emma Williams? She's located at your branch, correct?"

Fuck me. "Yes, she is."

"What are her stats?"

I clear my throat. "Forty-six manuscripts, five best sellers."

Gregory looks at me confused. "She sounds like an excellent candidate to me."

I nod, forcing a smile. "She's incredible."

Gregory's pen hits his pad and I grind my jaw. *Damn it.*

It's another hour and fifteen minutes before Gregory releases us from the meeting. Michael nudges me with his elbow as we stand from the conference table. "Want to go out for a drink?"

The tension in my head is like needles being stabbed into my skull repeatedly. "Yes. I could use one *or several*. Where to?"

"Lorraine's. It's a restaurant a couple doors down with a large drink selection and mouth-watering steaks."

"I'll be right there. I need to make a call to my office and check on things."

Michael waves. "I'll get us a table."

Entering the lobby of the Schmidt and Costello headquarters, there's a large, lengthy desk at the front, with a young, brunette secretary behind it, busy on her office phone. I take a seat in one of the brown, leather chairs by a giant leafy plant, using it as privacy. Pulling out my cell, I call Emma's office. She doesn't answer and disappointment greets me.

I begin dialing Rachel and think twice, and instead, I dial Claire's office and she picks right up.

"Where's Emma?"

"Grayson?"

"Yes. Where is she? She didn't answer her phone."

Recognizing my impatience, she gets right to business. "A local author stopped by to see her. He's in her office now. He brought her a thank you gift for all she's done for him."

My teeth grind. "What author?"

"Benjamin Luther."

"What did he bring her?"

"Flowers and a gift card, I think. At least that's what I could see when he walked in."

The sensation of needles stabbing my head is now a hammering. I'm irritated and I shouldn't be. "How are things in the office? How's Emma doing? Rachel giving her any trouble?"

Claire makes a sound as if she's suppressing a giggle. "Emma is doing great. She held a staff meeting yesterday and told everyone what she expected from them this week while you were away. Seems everyone is doing what they should be. Rachel and Emma had some words, but nothing came of it. Should I have Emma call you once Benjamin leaves?"

"No, I won't be available. I'll speak with her later. Thank you, Claire."

"Of course. How's the trip going?"

I rub my fingers over my temple. "It's going fine. Thank you for asking. I'll speak with you another time. I need to make a phone call."

"Talk soon. Take care," she replies.

I hang up and scroll through my contact list in search of the flower shop where I buy the white roses. I dial and the sweet old lady who runs it answers pleasantly. "Mary's Flowers, how can I help you?"

"Mary, it's Mr. Cole."

"Well hello, Mr. Cole. It's a pleasure to hear from you. What can I do for you today?"

Her caring, and friendly voice relieves some of my tension. "I'd like to order a dozen white roses and have them delivered tomorrow morning at eight a.m. Please place them in the most beautiful vase you have."

"Will do, Mr. Cole. Where would you like them delivered?"

"To Emma Williams. Sixth floor of the Wartburg building."

The noise of papers being moved around fills the background. "Would you like a message attached?"

I suppress my own laughter. Not one I want her to see. "No, thank you. I'll message her separately."

"Should I charge the card I have on record?"

"Yes. Thank you, Mary."

"My pleasure, Mr. Cole. Have a pleasant day."

Hanging up, I head to Lorraine's restaurant.

—EMMA—

Wednesday morning, I walk into my office and my jaw drops. Claire is behind me instantly, sneaking up like a ninja.

"I saw them delivered. I can take one guess who they're from."

Stepping farther into my office, I touch the petals of the roses. The blue fading to tan vase is stunning and the yellow bow gives it an extra touch. Bending down, I breathe them in. I can barely contain the joy I'm feeling. I turn to Claire and giggle.

"I was starting to feel like he'd forgotten about me. I drank four glasses of wine last night and fell asleep with my phone in my hand. I kept wanting to call or text him, but didn't want to seem needy."

Claire's cheeks puff out in laughter. "Em, I think he's just busy. He sounded stressed when I talked to him yesterday. I'm sure he would like it if you did call or text him."

My attention returns to the dozen white roses on my desk. "Well, now I have an excuse to call him." My forehead wrinkles at the recollection of Claire's comment. I turn to her. "You talked to him yesterday?"

"Yeah, he called to talk to you, but you were with Benjamin. I think he might have been jealous you got flowers from Ben."

My gaze sweeps to the tiny bouquet of colorful, assorted flowers hidden behind the long-stem white roses and a smile creeps along my face. "Did he?"

"Oh yeah, he didn't seem to like that at all. He got pretty short with me after I told him. He definitely has feelings for you, whether he wants to admit it or not."

"I'm gonna send him a quick text. Maybe I can catch him before they start their meeting."

Claire winks before heading back to her office.

Reaching into my purse, I dig out my phone and pull up Grayson's number.

I love them. Thank you.

I put my purse under my desk and turn on my computer before my phone dings.

Hopefully it makes up for me being gone and unable to leave you one each morning.

They do, but I'd rather have you here.

Miss me, Princess?

I do.

I've been thinking a lot about you too. I'm about to enter this meeting and won't be able to message you. I'd like to call you tonight.

Please do.

I'm giddy. So giddy, my leg is bouncing in the air. This man does crazy things to my head and heart. The last couple of days I buried myself in work as a distraction. I've missed him so much I've been walking around in a lovesick daze, but didn't want to be the one to make the first move. I wanted to know he missed me too. The dozen roses were a very clear message—he does.

Glancing at my clock, I realize the day has flown by. The book I read and made notes on helped keep my attention. Sending off a couple emails, I then shut down everything for the day. I smell the roses before gathering my purse and heading out the door.

On the way home, I pick up lasagna from Rosetta's and once home, I open a nice bottle of red to pair with it. A TV show keeps my attention while I anxiously wait for Grayson's call.

The TV is turned off and with the sun now set, I have the end table light on while I read for pleasure instead of work. I'm barely a few pages in when my phone rings.

"Grayson."

"Hi, Princess."

The sound of his voice instantly brings heat to my center.

"How's the meeting been?"

"Far less exciting than being at home with you."

I bite back my grin. "I'm looking forward to seeing you when you return."

"I'll be happy to see you too. Would you like to have dinner with me on Friday?"

"Yes."

"Have you thought a lot about me while I've been gone?"

"Probably too much."

"You didn't call or text me."

My cheeks flush. "I didn't want to bother you. I figured you were busy."

"I have been, but it hasn't stopped me from thinking about you."

"I like hearing you say that."

"What else would you like to hear?"

"What you thought about me."

"Do you want details?" His tone is sensual, challenging.

"I do."

"I'm thinking about you now, Emma, with my hand wrapped around my cock."

I let out a whimper of arousal.

"Do you like hearing that, Princess?"

"I do."

"Have you thought about us being intimate?"

Only every night. "Yes."

"Do something for me."

"What?"

"Slide your hand into whatever pretty lingerie you have on and touch yourself for me."

Nerves tickle my belly. Phone sex isn't something I'm experienced with, but I'm already wet from the thoughts of him stroking himself while thinking of me.

"Now, Princess. I'm gonna make you come while I'm on the phone."

Reaching down, I touch my clit and move in circles. As the warming sensation floods my body, I moan into the phone.

"That's it, Emma." His own breath quickens. "I know you're so wet for me. Imagine me inside you, moving in and out as you clench around me, soaking me as I fuck that sweet pussy."

My breathing is in sync with his and my strokes deepen as his words and voice milk my arousal.

"That's it, Emma, moan for me, remember how good it feels to have me inside you, filling you."

"Grayson…" his name escapes my parted lips as my orgasm takes control and owns me.

The slick sound of him fisting his cock slows. His moan fills my ear. I know he's come right along with me and it's got me all kinds of turned on.

"I love the way you sound when you come for me." His voice is sleepy, content.

My head is tilted back and my eyes are still closed as I come down from my high. "Grayson, you're hot as fuck."

He laughs into the phone. "I'll be home soon. You know what I want when I see you on Friday?"

I smile. "No panties?"

"That's right. I want full access to that pretty pussy of yours."

CHAPTER 15

GRAYSON

*I*T'S FRIDAY MORNING AND I'M relieved this week is over. As soon as my luggage is zipped, I sit on the hotel bed with my elbows on my knees and my thumbs cupped under my chin. As much as I don't want to admit it, not seeing Emma this week has been rough. I've been irritable and thought about her far too often. Even now, as I'm minutes away from taking a cab to the airport, my thoughts are of her and how I'll be arriving home earlier than expected, which gives me the opportunity to surprise her at work.

The hotel room phone rings. It's the front desk letting me know my cab has arrived.

A forty-five minute drive gets me to the airport. My first flight goes quickly, but the second is delayed. Taking a seat in the busy waiting area, I pull out my phone.

How's your day going?

Not fast enough. I'm anxious to see you.

How anxious?

Enough that I'm stealing work time thinking about you.
;)

The corner of my mouth lifts. This woman.

I enjoyed the pics you sent me last night. It gave me something to look forward to.

Liked them, did you?

I thought about how much I'd like to take that lingerie off you and put my mouth there instead.

I think we can arrange that. ;)

The attendant's voice crackles, then bellows from the speakers, announcing the plane will start boarding soon.

Got to go, Princess. Keep those thoughts going for me.

As soon as the plane lands, I gather my luggage and head home for a shower and a fresh suit. I plan to take Emma to Aqua again, before heading to her apartment to gather some of her things. I fully intend on keeping her at my condo this entire weekend. We have time to make up for.

While taking the elevator down to the garage, my mood has already lightened. The nagging headache that had been gnawing at my skull all week has dissipated.

The drive to the office takes far too long. I'm relieved when I arrive and quickly take the first spot I find in the parking garage. I walk down the block to the jeweler I called yesterday morning. As soon as I enter, I'm greeted by charming smiles.

I approach the nearest employee. "I'm Mr. Cole. I have an order I need to pick up."

"Of course. I'll have it to you momentarily."

The tall, young man in a blue suit similar to mine, walks to a door and disappears. He returns quickly, carrying a small, flat, red box. He opens it and displays it for me to see. I ordered the diamond and sapphire bracelet without having seen it. In person, it's more attractive than I expected. Satisfied, I smile and nod. "It's perfect."

The young man flashes a toothy grin and places it in a bag. "May I see the credit card you'd like to pay with, as well as your ID?"

"No bag is necessary," I reply as I remove my wallet from my pocket.

Payment and signature are completed and I ask for a gold bow for the box. The jeweler wraps it and hands the box to me.

Now I'm ready to see her. I tuck the box into the inside of my jacket and walk to the office.

The elevator dings as it arrives at our office floor and I enter the darkened lobby. No one is left save for one light. The light to Emma's office. A smile tilts my lips as I head to her door.

—EMMA—

I'M RUSHING TO GET these last few emails sent, so I can get home and get ready for dinner with Grayson. The sound of my office door opening startles me. I abruptly turn my chair to see who it is and shock overwhelms me. "Grayson."

"Hi, Princess. I got home early and wanted to surprise you."

I rush to him and he wraps his arms around me, then places two fingers beneath my chin and raises it. There's emotion in his eyes and I wonder if he's feeling even an inkling of what I am right now. I'm beyond thrilled to see him.

"I missed you."

His words are an arrow to my heart. Inside I'm waving the mercy flag. I surrender. Fucking take me now. Not waiting for a response, he claims my lips. The heat in his kiss weakens my knees. His grip tightens, holding me steady.

"I want to treat you to dinner and take you back to my place, but I don't think I can wait a moment longer to be inside you."

My hands hastily reach for the buttons of his jacket. "Then don't waste any more time." My lips crash into his as my fingers tuck under his jacket collar and slide it off his shoulders. The weight of the jacket leaves my hand as I toss it into the nearby chair.

With his seductive gaze set on me, he takes hold of my waist and backs me to the desk. Reaching around me, he presses the mute button. I laugh and he smothers my giggle with his smoldering kiss.

His lips burn like cinders across my neck as his hand touches my leg and traipses slowly up my thigh.

My grip is tight on the desk as arousal surges straight to my core. I'm ravenous for his touch and it escapes in my voice. "I've been waiting for this all week."

Damp lips leave a trail of sucks and nips across my collarbone as his free hand unbuttons my blouse.

"I'm rock hard, Emma, and I haven't even touched you yet. That's how much I want you."

The pressure of his fingers reaches my wet folds and a low groan escapes his lips and vibrates across my sensitive skin. "Always so ready for me." The feathered touch of his lips sweep across mine, heightening the desire scorching between my legs. "Tell me how much you want me, Emma. I want to hear you say it."

My head tilts back as my breast is pulled from my bra and my nipple sucked into his mouth. His tongue is a wicked device, drawing the words from my lips.

"I don't just want you, Grayson. I *need* you."

Skilled fingers plunge repeatedly, forcing my desire towards its peak. The caress of his mouth pulls my nipple between his lips before he withdraws, my arousal at a desperate state.

"Turn around, Princess. Put your hands on the desk and don't let go."

My body moves on its own volition—a puppet to his sensually promising words.

The moment my hands take hold of my desk his lips suck along my neck while his hands raise my skirt to my hips. I glance over my shoulder, pleased to get a glimpse of his steel erection. His hand wraps around it and with one hand on my hip, he thrusts into me.

Holding me by the waist, he slides me forward and back, working me over him. Greedy for the feel of him filling me, I move harder against him. Gripping my hair in his fist, he arches my back, tightens his hold and slams into me, tearing the moans from my lips.

A deep guttural moan breaks from him between the sound of my gratified cries. "You feel...so damn good."

"So do you."

Our eager bodies, longing for what we each desire, are relentless in our connection. Pushing and pulling, writhing over his cock, my moans flow together as my orgasm reaches a boiling point.

"Grayson," I sputter his name as my walls clench around him and I tremble through my orgasm.

One hard thrust fills me entirely as his cock swells and pumps into me. His grip loosens as his heated body leans over mine.

"I missed this, Emma. I missed this tight, little pussy of yours."

Licking his tongue along the shell of my ear prolongs the euphoric sensation pumping through me.

I move my hand into the one he has resting on the desk. His thumb grazes across my skin in unison with his tender kisses to my cheek, neck, and shoulder.

"I missed you so much this week," I admit.

I can feel him smile against my ear. "Stay with me this weekend?"

"The whole weekend?" I'm as surprised as I am excited.

"Yes, Emma. The *whole* weekend. Will you stay with me?"

"Yes."

He pulls out and I instantly miss the feel of him inside me.

I turn to face him and he raises my chin to kiss me. "Let's get cleaned up, Princess, so I can wine and dine my pretty girl."

Never in my life have such simple words made me feel so cherished. I wiggle my skirt down and then kiss him with all the passion held inside me.

As he directs his vehicle down Martin Street I quickly become aware of his destination. Aqua is in my sights and moments later he steers to the entrance. His hand grazes my bare knee. "This choice for dinner okay?"

I appreciate him asking because the thought of him spending that much on me again rattles my nerves.

"We could go somewhere less expensive unless you're set on eating here."

Raising his hand, his knuckle grazes my cheek and he smiles warmly at me. "I'm set on it, Princess. For you, price doesn't matter."

A giggle escapes me and his brows narrow in confusion.

"That was incredibly romantic, but it kind of made me sound like a hooker."

Grayson laughs, shaking his head. "It's never a dull moment with you."

Grinning, I shrug. "You adore me."

"That I do. Now get your fine ass out, Princess. The valet is waiting for you."

I quickly kiss his cheek, then step out. He joins me moments later and guides me inside with his hand on my lower back. The same hostess greets us and leads us to our table. As soon as we're settled, we order our drinks and look over the menu.

"Have you tried everything on this menu?" I ask, my gaze fixed on his handsome face and perfectly styled hair.

"Just about. Wondering about trying something you haven't before?"

"I am. I was thinking of trying the duck fesenjune."

"You won't regret that choice."

"Ok, I'm going with it."

A new waitress takes our orders. Surprisingly, this one doesn't know Grayson by name and for some reason, I'm glad she doesn't. After she leaves, Grayson reaches into his jacket and I get a glimpse of something red.

"I got you a present."

I barely contain my butt from wiggling in my chair. "You did?"

Grayson smiles, clearly humored. "I did." Reaching across the table, he places a small, red box in front of me.

I stare down at it, a little scared to see what's inside, already knowing how much he likes to spend on me.

"Open it, Princess. I'm looking forward to your reaction."

Carefully, I unwrap the bow and lift the top. My eyes widen and I try to capture my breath before it leaves me. In the box is a gorgeous bracelet with alternating sapphire and diamond stones.

"Oh my God, Grayson. This is beautiful!"

"Let me see it on you." Removing the bracelet from the box, Grayson fastens it around my wrist. My gaze transfixed, I'm mesmerized by the glimmering stones. Rubbing his thumb across my hand, Grayson asks, "You love it, don't you?"

Lifting my gaze to his, my eyes are teary. "It's a beautiful, incredible gift. Thank you."

He intertwines his fingers with mine. "I knew you'd be appreciative."

My lip quivers as I look at him. I'm full of so many different emotions. "I want to crawl in your lap and hug you."

"Save that thought, Princess. As soon as I have you

home, I want you in my lap with my cock buried deep inside you."

My face reddens as the waitress arrives. No doubt she heard him and I giggle. Grayson winks above his smirk.

We eat dinner quicker than usual and as we walk out of the restaurant, Grayson squeezes my ass and kisses my head before guiding me to the passenger side of his car.

Once inside the car, his hand takes mine and we ride content and quiet to my apartment.

As I enter my bedroom with my bathroom necessities in hand, I stop and laugh at the sight of Grayson removing all my underwear from my bag.

"What are you doing?"

"You won't be needing these."

"You know I do *like* to wear underwear," I reply, setting my toiletry bag on the bed.

"As long as you're at my condo, you won't be needing them." He winks and my body responds with a tingling sensation shooting straight to my vag.

My mind attempts to wander and I pull my thoughts back. "You're incorrigible, you know that?" I grab a pair of panties and stuff them back into the bag. "I'd like at least one pair, in case we go anywhere."

"All right. *One* pair."

I laugh and he grabs me and pulls me onto the bed with him, laying me above him. With a stroke of his hand, he affectionately rubs my cheek. "I'm glad I'm back here with you."

I search his eyes and see what could be adoration in them. He smiles and kisses me, making all thoughts scatter.

A swift slap on my ass jolts my eyes open. "Let's get the rest and get you back to my place."

CHAPTER 16

THE AROMA OF COFFEE PULLS me out of sleep. The sun shining in through Grayson's bedroom windows casts rays onto his bed, warming my uncovered legs. Removing the sheet from the parts of me it covers, I reach for his white, dress shirt near the bed. I slide it on and fasten a couple buttons, then follow the fragrance of crushed coffee grounds to the kitchen.

It's the second weekend I've spent at his condo since he returned from New York and I've learned his routine. He rises early, works out in the gym on the first floor, returns, showers, then starts coffee and waits for me to wake and either brings me breakfast or takes me out.

Entering the kitchen, I admire him in his khaki's and a long sleeve, gray shirt with his sexy tattoo peeking out of his rolled-up sleeves. He slides a coffee mug my direction and I move into his outstretched arm. "How'd you sleep?" he asks, before kissing my hair.

"Mmm, I'm gonna soak in the bath this morning. I'm still sore from last night."

His lip curls in some kind of alpha pride satisfaction. "You loved every bit of it, didn't you?"

I hide my grin behind the coffee mug and sip. "I did."

His warm lips brush along my cheek. "Wait 'til tonight. I have so much more in store for you."

My body tenses. "You planned on me staying over again?"

"Yes, why do you ask?" His brows crease and he removes his arm from around me for a clearer view of my face.

"You said you had some work to do today and Megs asked me to go shopping, then go out with her tonight."

"Where does she want to go?"

"Dinner then drinks and dancing at Sin."

The tightening of his jaw lets me know he's not happy.

"Grayson, you have nothing to worry about."

"Will you come back here after?" His tone has lost the light sensuality it had moments ago.

"Maybe, depending on whether or not Megs wants to stay at my place."

He nods, seeming to accept my response. Affectionately he strokes his hand down my back, then lowers and grips my ass, pulling my body flush against his. His kiss comes quick and unexpectedly. Riding along the edge of his lips is unbridled passion. I set my mug on the counter, before I drop it, and give into his head-spinning kiss.

When he separates his lips from mine, I realize I'm gripping him as though he's an anchor, keeping my body in place, while my mind and emotions are lost in a sea of our desire.

"That's to remind you of what you're missing out on." His palm swats my ass. "Now go have fun with your girlfriend."

"Grayson!" I rub my cheek, knowing full well that's gonna leave a mark.

He glances over his shoulder on the way to his office and smirks. "That'll teach ya, Princess."

"Teach me what?"

"To choose a night out dancing with Megan over me."

"You're being awfully pouty about it."

"Damn straight I am." His voice carries down the hall as he disappears into his home office.

I laugh as I pick up my coffee. Looks like I'll be getting breakfast on my own this morning.

Carrying the warm mug in my hand, I walk past his office and he glances at me. I giggle at his mopey expression.

"Keep giggling, Emma and I'll tie you to my bed and you won't be going anywhere."

"That sounds like a delicious promise, not a threat," I shout back.

"Emma, come back to my office. *Right now.*"

Beneath his serious demand, I can hear the playful sensuality. Anticipating what he has in store, I turn back and stop at his office door.

"Yes, Boss?" I ask, playfully.

His lip quirks. "Come here."

I set the mug on his desk and take slow, casual steps to him. His hand reaches out and grazes the outside of my thigh then tightens on my ass. "You know I'm having a hard time letting you go, right?"

"I do."

Reaching inside his borrowed shirt, his hands skim along my waist. Between the opening of the fabric, his lips leave a tantalizing, damp kiss on my stomach. "I selfishly want you here with me. I don't like the thought of another man dancing with you."

Another kiss lower on my abdomen tempts my arousal. "I won't be dancing with anyone, but Megan."

"Inhibitions drop when alcohol is involved."

Another kiss just above my clit tips my head back and forces my lids closed. "I won't have more than a couple drinks."

"You're a beautiful woman, Emma. Men will be salivating to have a taste of you."

The touch of his tongue against my clit takes my breath. "You're the only one I want to taste or touch me."

"I believe you, Emma. That's the only reason I'm letting you go."

My hands clench in his hair as his erotic kiss draws a moan from my lips.

WITH IT BEING SATURDAY NIGHT, the dance bar is packed. Megan and I maneuver through the busy crowd, find a small high-top table and order our drinks. Seeing lovers dancing on the floor just adds to me missing Grayson. I'm happy to be out with Megan. I haven't seen her much since Grayson got back, but still part of me would rather be back at his condo with him.

As the memories of this morning tickle my thoughts, my thighs rub together. I laugh aloud as my finger swirls the straw of my Mojito. "It almost feels odd wearing underwear. I practically never wear them anymore because of Grayson's panty-less fetish."

Megan pulls her attention from her man-hunting and smirks. "Your boyfriend is a kinky freak."

Hearing Megs say boyfriend sounds odd. It's been three weeks and we still haven't established exactly what we are. Perhaps Megan is right and I should start considering Grayson my boyfriend.

"That he is and I love that about him."

She laughs and takes a drink of her pink Margarita.

I admire the curls in her hair as she looks back over the crowd.

"You ready to dance?" she asks eagerly.

"Sure, but I promised Grayson I'd only dance with you."

She winks. "We'll see how long that lasts." She waves her hand at my drink. "Hurry and finish."

I suck the remaining liquid down and before setting the glass on the table, she's already taken my hand, tugging me onto the dance floor. "You already see someone you're interested in, don't you?"

"Mm, hmm."

"Once he joins us, I'm getting off the dance floor."

"All right," Megan replies, sounding disappointed.

Thankfully the alcohol has given me a confidence boost. With it, I'm a graceful swan; without it, I probably look like a flapping fish out of water. Megan, on the other hand, is an amazing dancer. She loves to dance every chance she gets. When she settles down it needs to be with someone who loves to dance as much as she does. I can go either way. I enjoy it, but every time I've come out dancing with Megan it was to have a good time with her and to meet guys. Well now I've met one and he's all I can think about as my best friend eye fucks the man she's interested in getting to know.

Like a wolf stalking its prey, the redheaded fella comes right toward Megan. *Shit, I've lost my dance partner already.* My shoulders drop and I head back to our table. I order another drink then pull out my cell phone. My mood brightens when I see a text waiting for me from Grayson.

How's your night going, Princess?

It's ok. I miss you.

How much?

Like debating leaving now and coming to your place miss you.

What if I'm not there?

My stomach instantly aches as if a chain is being tightened around it.

You're not home?

No, Princess. I'm not.

Where are you?

Somewhere where I have a good view of you.

You're here at Sin?

Just arrived. Want to find me?

YES!! :)

Start looking. I'm waiting here for you.

My head jerks around in search of Grayson. It isn't easy to locate anyone with the lights so dim and the mess of people moving around. Wait! He said he has a good view of me. I glance up. The stairs to the loft. I start walking and my phone vibrates in my hand.

Getting warmer, Princess.

I reach the steps and anticipation replaces my worry. A grin spreads across my face as I take the steps as quickly as my heels will allow. As soon as I'm on flat ground, I search the tables and booths. My phone vibrates again.

So close, yet so far.

Moving farther in, I search the booths along the wall. The very last one is where I find him. He's leaning against the wall, a scotch in his hand and dressed impeccably with looks that can kill. He looks like a freaking James Bond character come to life. The corner of his mouth lifts into a lascivious grin. "Now that you found me, what are you going to do with me?"

I crawl into the booth and straddle him. My internal naughty girl is all kinds of turned on by this game. I kiss him and he squeezes my ass, pressing me into him.

"I think you should take me home, *right now*."

Grayson bites his lip and releases it. That tiny action lights my arousal on fire. Stroking my face, the smoldering look in his eyes tells me he's just as turned on.

"Why wait until we're home?"

My body tingles with excitement. "Are you saying we should have sex *here*, *now*?"

"Won't take much for it to happen."

His free hand reaches under my dress, moves my underwear to the side and kneads my throbbing clit. I move against his touch, wanting more. "You want it, don't you, Princess? You want my cock in you?"

"Yes, I do."

His thumb presses my bottom lip before he pulls my face to his and kisses me with aggressive need. My body is ignited. Every nerve buzzing. His kinkiness is reaching a new level and I'm extremely aroused.

With pleasured strokes, his fingers ready me for him. "Unzip my pants, Emma."

Wasting no time, I do as instructed, then reach in and pull out his length. I stroke him twice as he tongue-fucks my mouth. My body is screaming with need. I want him bad. Raising myself on my knees, just enough to put his tip to my opening, I slide down on him and we both release a fulfilled breath. Taking my ass in his hands, he rocks me over him, riding this high with me.

STILL IN THE BOOTH, Grayson's lips nibble my ear as he plays with the bracelet on my wrist. "I like that you haven't taken it off since I gave it to you."

Lowering my drink, I turn my head to face him and kiss him. "Why would I? I love it."

"I know you do and that means a lot to me."

I rub his leg and he pulls me tighter against him.

"I'm glad it does."

"You ready to go back to my place?"

"Let me check on Megan first."

Grayson frowns before lifting the scotch and

downing the remainder of it. I'm beginning to feel like Megan bothers him. "Do you not like Megan?"

His hand touches my back and rubs affectionately. "I don't like that she brought you along while she's looking to get laid."

Irritation tickles my chest. "Is that why you came? To make sure I didn't do anything?"

"I came because I wanted to see you, and yes, I wanted to make sure you didn't run into any trouble."

"What kind of trouble?"

"Like a man trying to take you home with him."

"I could've shut that down on my own."

"Yes, you could've, but with me here, you didn't have to."

"Mm, hmm, I feel like maybe I should be mad at you for being all macho possessive, but yet, I'm not. I'm glad you showed up to hang out with me. You made it more fun." I wink and he grins.

"All right, Princess. Go see if Megan is going home with you, so I can be selfish and take you home with me."

With his hand on my back, we walk down to the main floor and search for Megan. We find her at a circular booth with the redhead from earlier. I slide in next to her and she kisses my cheek. She quickly notices Grayson and her expression reveals her surprise.

Grayson and redhead are shaking hands and making introductions while Megan leans into my ear. "He showed up here?"

My smile widens. "He did. He wanted to hang out with me *and* make sure I didn't get scooped up by another man."

Her rosy cheeks puff out as she smirks. "Wow, Boss man has a jealous streak," she quips.

"Don't tell him that. He'll deny it. Honestly though, I'm glad he came, I wasn't having a good time."

With a pouty lip, she frowns. "You weren't?"

I rub her leg, soothing her worry. "Not because of you. You found someone to hang with and get to know. It made me miss Grayson. I didn't want to hang out with anyone else."

"I get it. Honestly. I'm envious you have a guy so smitten with you. Are you two leaving?"

"I think so." I glance at Grayson and redhead. They seem to be chumming it up pretty well, but when Grayson's eyes catch mine I know what he's thinking. I'm thinking it too—us at his place—alone. I turn my attention back to Megan. "You ok with that? Or do you want us to stay?"

She glances at red, then back at me and grins. "I'm good. I think I'm gonna have a long night with Jordan."

I reach around and hug her. "Be careful and if you need *anything*, call or text and I'll come get you, *no matter where you are*."

"I know you will. Have fun with your Boss boyfriend. I want to hear all the details later." She winks and it draws a smile from my lips.

"Bye, babe." I stand and Grayson says his goodbye to Jordan, then puts his arm around my back as we leave.

CHAPTER 17

EMMA

THE REST OF THE WEEKEND with Grayson was incredible and it makes up for the three dozen emails waiting for me on Monday. Cringing at the sight of them, I call Lisa.

"Lisa, do you have any idea why I have at least two dozen submissions in my email?"

"Oh shoot! I'm so sorry. I uploaded Schmidt and Costello on a new agency site and I must have added your email instead of mine. I'll get that fixed right away. Do you mind sending me all those submissions so I can go through them for you?"

I let out a breath. "Yeah, it'll take me a bit to go through and forward each one. Thanks for correcting that."

"Of course. Sorry about that."

"It's all right."

I hang up and begin the process of sorting through

and forwarding the emails. A knock on my office door pulls me from my concentration.

"Miss Williams?"

I turn my gaze and I'm startled to see Arnold Cole standing in my office looking dapper in his navy suit and shiny, peppered hair.

"Mr. Cole." I immediately stand. "What can I do for you?"

"It seems my son won't do me the honors of asking you to dinner with us, so I had to stop in here myself."

"Dinner?"

His lip curls and I recognize that smile. It's Grayson's. "Your birthday is this week, is it not?"

"Grayson told you?" I'm completely surprised by this.

"Not exactly. When he declined to have dinner with me this Friday I asked him why and he said he was busy...with you, Miss Williams. So I had my secretary do a little digging and she easily discovered that your birthday is the day after. I thought it would be worthwhile to get to know the woman my son seems to have such a significant interest in."

I think it's far more than a significant interest at this point, but I have no desire to be childish with this man and squabble over terms.

"Sure, dinner sounds lovely."

He nods, clearly pleased. "We'll go to Bellini's Fine Italian. Seven o'clock."

"Perfect."

"Would you mind keeping this between you and me

for now? My son might try to talk you out of it and I would be terribly disappointed."

"Disappointed by what?" Grayson's tone is harsh as he approaches behind Arnold. He closes my office door and crosses his arms, waiting for an answer.

Arnold smirks at Grayson. "If she declined my invitation to have dinner with us this Friday. Sweet Emma has already accepted."

Grayson's eyes narrow and I feel the tension building in the room.

"Dinner with both of us?" Grayson repeats.

"I thought it would be nice to get to know the woman that is keeping my son's attention these days."

The way he says the last few words makes my skin crawl. There seems to be an underlying message and I don't like being ignorant of it.

Grayson's jaw ticks. He's obviously irritated, but he's doing his best to remain calm. "Where are we having dinner?"

"Bellini's Fine Italian, seven o'clock."

"We'll see you then. Unfortunately, Emma has work she needs to get back to and she can't continue to chat."

Arnold nods, giving me a pleasant smile. "Of course. It was a pleasure speaking with you, Emma. I look forward to seeing you on Friday."

As Grayson walks his father out, I sit back in my chair and let out the breath I had been holding. Grayson returns moments later and closes the door once again. His gaze is steady on mine.

"How long was Arnold here?"

"A few minutes."

"Did you talk about anything else other than dinner plans?"

"No. Is everything okay?"

"No, I don't appreciate him coming into my workplace and cornering you like that."

"I didn't feel cornered. I was surprised is all. Were you coming into my office to tell me something?"

Grayson rubs the back of his neck. He seems distant in thought. "I need to have a meeting with Rachel. We'll be in my office for a while with the windows shaded."

"Oh." Jealousy strikes and I look out the window, hiding it.

"Emma."

Turning my head to face him, I know he sees it.

"There's nothing for you to be jealous about."

"I still don't like it."

"I know, Princess." His voice softens and his focus returns, narrowing in on me. "That's why I came to tell you. It's just business."

"What business?"

"Emma, I'm still your Boss. I can't share everything with you. You trust me, don't you?"

I grumble beneath my breath. He knows I do. "Yes."

"All right. I'll take you to lunch afterward to make up for it."

"I like the sound of that."

"It'll be an extra long lunch." He winks and my body warms with anticipation.

"That's even better."

WITH IT BEING MY BIRTHDAY week, I thought I'd be giddier now that it's Friday, but actually I'm exhausted. This week has been insanely busy; the last several manuscripts I sent to publishers have all been turned down, my mother has been texting me to call her, and I'm dreading having that conversation, and on top of it all, Grayson has been getting grumpier as the week progressed. I think we're both ready for a stiff drink and I'm particularly ready for his stiff cock.

After shutting down my computer, I lean in and smell the white roses from this week and then close my office door behind me. When I enter Grayson's office he's in full concentration mode, typing away. It's not until I set my purse down on the chair and move to his side of the desk that his attention transitions to me.

Reaching out, he pulls me into his lap. "You're a sight for sore eyes."

When I kiss him, I don't sense his usual calm, confident demeanor. He seems tense.

"It's been a rough week for you too, huh?"

"It has and I'm not thrilled about this dinner with Arnold." His finger plays with the button of my blouse, threatening to pop it open. "I'd rather be taking you home with me and getting started on spoiling you all weekend for your birthday."

While running my fingers through his hair, I give a little tug and he bites his lip. That reaction of his is my weakness. I get wet just watching it. Lowering my hand, I place it over his pants and caress him. He lets out a gratified breath. "I'm sure the spoiling will commence immediately after dinner, until then, I'd like to spoil you a little."

With a flick of his finger, my button is unfastened and he's opening my blouse for a better view of my breasts. "I haven't had you since Monday, Princess. That's too damn long."

Sliding out of his arm, I squat on my knees in front of him and he watches me with interest in his eyes. "I agree. It's been far too long." Unzipping his pants, I release his erection. He leans his head back on the chair as I lower my mouth onto him.

His hand winds in my hair and he moans a satisfied breath as I suck harder and take more of him. "Damn, Emma, this is what I needed."

Grayson leans forward and tightens his grip on my hair when I hum with my sucking. "You dirty little Princess."

Gathering more of my hair in his hand, he moves it so he can watch me. Seeing the desire in his eyes and the satisfaction on his face heightens my own arousal. I reach down between my legs and low hiss escapes him. "You need me, don't you?"

"Mm, hmm," I mumble.

Using my hair, he pulls me off him, lifts me onto his desk, shoves my skirt up my legs, and thrusts into me. His kiss smothers my cry of satisfaction.

The desk rocks as he slams into me, his hips thrusting in unison with mine. My ass sticks to paperwork and I slide across the surface as cries and moans spill from my lips. His tight grip in my hair adds to the pleasure he's creating between my legs.

"Don't stop," I cry out.

"Not going to, Princess. Not until you come for me."

The slick sound of us coming together is drowned out by my release. As I clench around him, he lets out his own satisfied groan.

Touching his sweat-beaded forehead to mine, his breath feathers my lips. "You make everything better."

"So do you." The way he's looking at me now has me completely smitten. Those *I love you* words are starting to creep into my mind, but I'm hesitant to say them. It doesn't feel like the right time.

"You sure you don't want to skip this dinner and let me take you to my place and draw a bath for you?"

"Oh, you know how to tempt me, Grayson Cole. It's too late to cancel, but I'm holding you to that bath. I want it after dinner."

He pulls out from me and I whimper.

Leering at me, he tucks himself back into his pants. "That sound you make every time I pull out makes me want to fuck you all over again."

The corner of my mouth curls into a lascivious grin. "Please do."

His knuckle swipes under my chin, slightly lifting my gaze. "You are my dirty little Princess, aren't you?"

"That I am."

Grayson helps me down from his desk and tugs on my skirt. "I'll be at your place at six to pick you up."

"I'll be ready."

"Emma." Grayson lifts my chin again to meet his gaze. His expression immediately tells me he means business. "Wear underwear tonight. At least to dinner."

I giggle and Grayson frowns. "Of course I'm wearing underwear while having dinner with you father. Now stop fussing over me so I can go home and get ready."

Cupping my face, he kisses me. "See you soon."

Opening the passenger door, Grayson helps me out of the car.

"Did I mention how good you look?" He asks, hugging me close to him as walk to the entrance of Bellini's.

"You did when you arrived, but I like hearing it. Tell

me as much as you want." I wink and he gives me that charming smile that makes my heart flutter.

Entering the dimly lit red and yellow restaurant, the cute brunette hostess greets us with a pleasant smile. Grayson gives his name and she quickly guides us to our table. Arnold stands, pulls a chair out for me, placing me between them.

"You look lovely, Emma," Arnold compliments with an added smile.

Grayson's gaze whips to him and his eyes darken.

Was that a silent threat I just witnessed? "Thank you," I reply cordially.

Thankfully, the waiter's arrival cuts the awkward tension.

After our drink orders are placed and the waiter tells us the specials, he leaves and I turn my attention to the menu.

"Emma, how do you like working for my son?"

Setting down the menu, I meet his curious gaze.

"I love working for him. Even if we weren't dating, I still would. He has great management skills and is efficient at his job."

Arnold nods and grins. "How long have you and Grayson been *dating*?" He glances at Grayson, then back at me.

"A month," I reply, suddenly feeling self-conscious. I don't even know why I'm feeling this, maybe because Grayson and I still haven't talked about what we are. All the boxes check off for being a couple though; only seeing each other, sex and intimacy, spending all our free time together, he bought me a diamond and sapphire bracelet. What doesn't say *you're my girl* like a thousand-dollar bracelet? Even Megan called him my boyfriend.

My heart starts pumping rapidly as Grayson appears tense while looking over the menu. He's irritated. Why is he irritated? Is it what I said? This dinner is quickly becoming an epic failure.

When the waiter brings my wine, I sip several times trying to take the edge off my unease. The young man takes our orders and as soon as he's gone, Arnold's attention once again returns to me.

"That's a lovely bracelet you're wearing. Was it a gift from Grayson?"

Now I feel like a damn child under scrutiny. My cheeks burn and I know the blood is rushing to my skin, revealing how uncomfortable I am.

"Yes, it was a gift," Grayson responds. His gaze now meeting Arnold's.

"Excuse me. I'm going to the lady's room." I scurry away from the table, needing some distance from the awkward tension. This dinner is not going how I imagined.

Inside the bathroom, I take a breath and dab my face with a wet towel. Finding an empty stall, I use it, then wash up and gain the courage to return to our table. Stepping into the hallway, a hand grabs my wrist and I instinctively jump. Arnold releases my wrist, quickly closes the space between us, pinning me against the wall.

His fierce blue eyes center on mine. I try to move farther back, but there's nowhere to go.

"You're a lovely woman, Emma." His hand grazes my jaw. "You seem to have captured my son's affections. I can't help wondering if you and I would have just as much fun."

Vomit rises to my throat and I push his hand away. "I'm not interested in whatever you're offering."

He shrugs. "It wouldn't be the first time Grayson and I shared a woman. If he's okay with it, you should be too."

Tears prickle my eyes and my body tenses, wanting out of this situation as soon as possible. The things he's saying are churning my stomach and ripping a hole into my heart.

"I'm not Grayson's plaything and I have no interest in being one for you," I snap.

"How much?"

"What do you mean?"

Arnold touches the bracelet on my wrist. "How much would it cost for you?"

I'm staring at this man I thought deserved my respect. Now I couldn't be any more disgusted. Placing my hand on his chest, I shove him back. "You're a fucking pig."

He grabs my wrist as I bolt to leave. "Stop pretending to be insulted. We both know Grayson has no intention of having something serious with you. If you believe that, you're a foolish girl."

Yanking my wrist from his grasp, my bracelet snaps

and tings as it lands on the floor. As tears trickle down my cheeks, I scoop it up, before running out of the restaurant.

—GRAYSON—

THE FOOD HAS BEEN DELIVERED and I'm about to go check on Emma when I see Arnold returning to the table. He sits down with a smug expression and my gut tightens.

"Where's Emma?"

"She left."

I grind my teeth. "Why?"

Adjusting his jacket, he takes a drink of his Bourbon. "The silly girl thought she meant something to you."

"*What* did you say to her?"

He shrugs and I barely refrain from crossing the table and slugging the smug smirk off his face.

"I offered her the same thing you are."

"You made a sexual advance toward her?"

"Yes, isn't that all she is Grayson? A new flavor of the month?"

My hand slams down on the table. "Fuck you, Arnold. She's more than that."

"I did you a favor, Son. I got rid of her before your feelings became more involved. It's bound to end one way and I'd rather see her brokenhearted over you than the other way around." He puts back the remainder of his drink and clicks his tongue as though what he did was justifiable and actually for my benefit.

My eyes narrow on his. "Evelyn broke you all those years ago and instead of dealing with it, you became a heartless womanizer and turned me into the same damn thing. Emma didn't deserve to be treated like that. She's not like the others." I pull out my wallet and toss cash onto the table. "Don't do me any more favors, Arnold or I'll ensure some of your more private dealings find their way into a reporter's hands."

I stand to leave and he taps his glass and nods at my seat. "Sit down, Son. We need to talk about this."

Seeing the fear in his eyes, I know it has nothing to do with losing his son. He only cares about two things; himself and his business. "There's nothing more for us to talk about."

As I walk out of the restaurant, I immediately dial Emma. I hate knowing she's out there alone, hurting over me, or what my father said to her. She doesn't pick up and the ringing goes to her voicemail.

"Damn it!"

I jump in the car and head to her apartment.

—EMMA—

I KNEW THE FIRST PLACE Grayson would look for me was my apartment, so after a tear-soaked cab ride, I came to Masco's for a drink—or four. The bartender keeps giving me sympathetic glances. Even after using the bathroom to clean up my makeup, my face is still red and puffy from crying so hard. Downing the rest of my shot, I pull my phone out to call Megan.

Looking at the screen, I see I have six missed calls from Grayson and three texts. I open them and read.

Emma, where are you?

Call me. I'm worried about you. We need to talk.

I'm sorry for what happened tonight. Please call me.

As I read his texts messages more tears sting my eyes. I don't want to see him. I don't want him to admit that his father is right and that all I am is a plaything. I set the phone down and fiddle with the broken bracelet in my hand. I can't believe it. I don't want to believe it. I know I mean something to him.

I motion to the bartender for another shot. Bringing my hand back to my side I notice a woman enter the bar who looks familiar. I wipe away a stray tear and narrow my focus. It's Olivia. *Fuck me, why now?*

She blinks a couple times as she stares at me, then

with one perfect, high-heeled, foot after the other, she approaches.

"Emma, right?"

She sits on the stool next to me as I sniffle and nod. "Yeah."

"You look awful. Did Grayson end things? I remember when he ended it with me. That was a rough night for me, too."

"No, he didn't end things."

"Oh, I apologize. That was presumptuous. Is it anything you'd like to talk about?"

I shake my head. Why is she being so nice to me?

"Those tears are for Grayson, though, aren't they?"

I blink back more tears.

"I think there's something you need to know about Grayson."

With her pretty, pink nail-polished hand, she motions for the bartender and I look at her expectantly. "What do I need to know?"

Meeting my gaze, I can see empathy in her eyes. "Grayson is the kind of man who wants to own you; heart, body and soul and once you've given him everything, once you're conquered, he'll lose interest. It's best you get out now."

"And you're not just trying to scare me off? I saw the way you were chumming it up with him the last time we were here. You seemed very interested in rekindling things."

"What can I get you, darling?" the bartender asks, interrupting.

"A chocolate Margarita." Her attention returns to me. "I know better than to have any feelings for Grayson. I learned my lesson. I was simply looking for sex. He is especially good at it, as I'm sure you know."

I fight back the vomit burning my throat.

Flicking her raven hair over her shoulder, she tilts her head as she looks at me. "As a woman who's been where you are, I'm trying to do the decent thing and warn you before your heart gets broken. Grayson isn't capable of loving you or any woman. He knows how to make a woman feel amazing, but will never be able to give you everything you need emotionally."

Grabbing my shot glass, I raise it, downing it in one gulp. "People change," I respond, setting the empty glass down.

"Men like Grayson don't change. He's a creature of habit. You'll see. The moment he realizes you love him, he'll end it."

The bartender brings her Margarita and I ask for another shot.

"How many is that?" Olivia asks.

I shrug. "Fifth or Sixth?"

She takes out her cell phone and busies herself while happily sipping from her straw. I've never wanted to punch a woman so much in my life and yet, part of me respects her for giving me the fair warning. She has a past with Grayson and as gut-wrenching as it is, she seems to know him better than I do.

—GRAYSON—

PACING ACROSS MY FLOOR, RUNNING my hand over my neck, the tension builds. I don't know Megan's number or where she lives. Emma hasn't returned to her apartment. She could be anywhere with *anyone*. I knew I never should've let the dinner happen.

My phone buzzes in my hand and I immediately slide the screen to read the text.

Grayson, it's Olivia. Emma is at Masco's. If you care about this woman, you should come get her. She's several shots in and not looking good.

I'll be right there. Don't let her leave.

Grabbing my keys, I'm out the door in seconds.

Entering the bar, I spot Olivia and Emma right away. Olivia is rubbing Emma's shoulder as Emma wipes away her own tears. Seeing her like this kills me. My chest aches in discomfort. I approach slowly and pull a hundred-dollar bill from my wallet. I move between Olivia and Emma and toss the bill on the bar, setting her empty glass on it.

"You're coming home with me."

"Grayson." She stares at me, her eyes glossy and puffy, seeming to struggle with my presence as if she dreamt me up.

Reaching out, I stroke her cheek and she leans into

my touch, giving me a minuscule amount of relief. "I'm here and I'm taking you home with me."

Her lip quivers before she speaks. "My birthday is tomorrow. I don't want to spend it with you anymore."

With my thumb, I wipe away a stray tear. "Emma, you're drunk. Come home with me. I'll take care of you."

"Will you take me home? I want to go back to my apartment."

"Yes." I take her hand and she moves off the barstool, her shoulders slumped and her eyes weary. Putting my arm around her waist, I hold her close. I give a nod to Olivia. "Thanks."

She nods back and watches with curiosity and confusion in her eyes. I'm sure she's surprised to see me. She herself had called me drunk and crying, and I told her to call a friend. I'm such an asshole.

I place Emma into the passenger seat and see her lids are heavy. Taking off my jacket, I place it around her. She nestles into the leather seat and closes her eyes. I look over at her when I get in. She looks tired, sad, and helpless. I can't leave her at her apartment to wake up alone and miserable on her birthday, so I head to my condo.

Carrying her inside the lobby attracts attention, but I don't care. I nod to onlookers as I press the elevator's close door button. She's asleep in my arms, peaceful and trusting. How different this night could have turned out if I'd kept her away from Arnold. All she wanted was a nice birthday dinner with her boyfriend and his father. What she got instead was a man who fears commitment and his chauvinistic, narcissistic father.

Holding her in my arms, I struggle to put the key in the door. I manage to get through with her only stirring slightly. A ting sound comes from my feet and I look down. The bracelet I bought her is lying broken on the floor.

I gently move it with my foot, so I can close the door behind us. Carrying her to my room, I place her on my bed and remove her heels and dress. Down to her lingerie, I tuck her into the blankets and she stirs.

"Grayson, am I home?"

I stroke her cheek as her words clench my chest. "Yes, Princess. You're home."

CHAPTER 18

EMMA

WHEN I WAKE UP MY skull feels like little goblins snuck in through my ears and are hammering on the walls of my brain. That's how bad my hangover hurts. On Grayson's night stand is a tall glass of water, aspirin, and a black, flat box with a small box on top of it, both wrapped in gold bows, but he's nowhere to be found. I go for the aspirin and water then bring the boxes in front of me and untie the bows. The top box is filled with a stunning pair of diamond and sapphire earrings that match my broken bracelet. *Shit! Where is my bracelet?* Panic sets in and I move off the bed and search through my dress, shoes, and purse. I can't find it.

The sound of the front door opening causes my nerves to splinter. *Damn it! Why am I at his condo?* Hurrying, I put my dress and shoes on, then sit on the edge of his bed and open the second box. My bracelet, it's fixed! I let out a breath of relief and my heart skips a beat. He had my bracelet fixed and got me matching earrings. My emotions swirl in my belly and nausea threatens to turn to vomit. I'm so confused right now and this hammering headache is not helping. I hate you, Jose Cuervo.

The smell of food churns my stomach even more. Seriously, today is my birthday and I could not feel any more miserable. There's only one thing I can do to begin feeling better. Rushing to Grayson's bathroom, I close the door before he enters his bedroom.

I turn the shower to hot and within minutes the room is steamy. Stepping in, I immediately feel soothed by the warm water running over my body. My tight muscles begin to unwind. Reaching for whatever shampoo he has, my hand stops mid-reach. My body wash! He bought my body wash! I snatch it up like an old teddy bear I just re-discovered and scrub myself head-to-toe.

Hearing the bathroom door open, my relaxed muscles tighten all over again.

"Emma?"

"You bought my body wash!"

I can't see him, but I'm pretty sure he just smiled when I hear his tone change. "I did."

"You fixed my bracelet too?"

"I have it under warranty. The jeweler replaced the whole bracelet."

"And you got me earrings."

He crosses the bathroom until he's just outside the shower door.

"I did. Do you like them?"

"Of course. I love them."

The door slides open several inches. He looks me over and his sexy as fuck grin lifts the corner of his mouth and my body tingles.

"I wanted to be the first to tell you happy birthday."

My cheeks grow warm as I smile. "Thank you, Grayson."

His hand grips the shower door and he eyes me like he's struggling to keep from joining me. "We have things to talk about, Princess, but they can wait. Today is your birthday and I want you to enjoy it. I brought fresh clothes from your apartment for you to change into. After breakfast, we have somewhere to go."

I grimace as my stomach churns. "I don't think I can eat."

"Even if it's just a couple bites it will help you feel better."

"All right, I'm almost finished. Just need to wash my hair."

"I'll be waiting for you."

He closes the door and it breaks me. Our dynamic has clearly shifted. Ordinarily, he'd have joined me in the shower and pinned me against the wall. Now it feels like we're walking on eggshells around each other.

Finishing my shower, I see he left my toiletry bag sitting on the sink with everything I need inside. Brushing my teeth rids me of any remaining unclean feeling. A blow dry and light makeup has me feeling presentable. In his room, my bag is on the bed with a few clothing options. I wonder how early he got up to do all this. Glancing at the clock on his nightstand, I laugh. It's 10:13. He's had plenty of time to run around while I slept off my hangover. How embarrassing.

Wearing skinny jeans and a sweater, I grab my bags up, tidy his bed, and head to the kitchen. When I set my bag by the door, I notice he's watching and he seems disappointed. Oddly, I didn't even consider staying the night. He probably expected I would.

He pushes the glass of orange juice toward me as I join him at the breakfast table in his kitchen. A plate with a waffle and strawberry topping is waiting for me.

"You got my favorite."

His eyes crinkle as he smiles. "I did."

"You're going all out today, aren't you?"

He laughs and I wonder what I don't know yet. "I have something special planned for you that I know you'll love."

I let out a breath. "Are you doing all this because you feel bad about what your father did or because you want to?"

He glances out the window then back at me. "The truth is both."

"I know you don't want to talk about it yet, but I think we should. It's the elephant in the room and I want to clear it out."

Grayson sets down his fork and leans back in his chair. "All right. Start with telling me everything he said to you. Don't leave anything out."

I stop twirling the fork in my hand and set it down.

I take a breath and then retell Grayson everything in detail, from the moment I stepped out of the bathroom to when I ran out of the restaurant in tears.

By the time I've finished, his eyes are glazed over and he's clearly angry. His jaw is locked and he's running his hand over the back of his neck. Crossing his arms, he looks out the window in thought and I admire his strong jaw, tightly pinched with the emotions he's holding onto. Looking back at me, there's so much emotion in his eyes that it's difficult for me to decipher exactly how he feels. "Emma, I'm sorry he treated you like that. To explain why he did, I think it's time I share my past with you."

Setting down the orange juice after taking a sip, I try to calm my rattled nerves. "Ok."

Still leaning back in his chair, he rests an elbow on the table. "When I was ten, my father caught my mother having an affair. Walked right in on her bent over the desk of his business partner. Before the affair, my father was madly in love with her. Finding her with another man broke him; he divorced her and made sure she received absolutely nothing, including me. She moved in with my aunt and I never heard from her again, which I imagine was his doing. After the divorce, he changed, became bitter and misogynistic.

"Every woman he dated after was a toy, something to conquer, then toss aside. His way of thinking is, break their hearts before they can break yours. Growing up, I was a shy teenager, always had my head in books. At eighteen, he hired a prostitute to help me lose my virginity. Said I needed to learn how to seduce a woman so I could get what I wanted from them before they took what they wanted from me."

My throat's so dry I raise the orange juice and take another sip. "Did you have sex…with the prostitute?" I ask, nervously.

Grayson shakes his head. "No, I was too scared back then. I'd never even touched a girl before that day. She gave me oral and then I paid her to tell my father we'd had sex. I lost my virginity to a woman in college." The sun gives a golden glow to Grayson's face as he looks out the window, his thoughts miles away from the here and now. "Her name was Danielle and I loved her. I wanted to marry her, but she broke my heart when I caught her cheating. My father gloated, gave me the *I told you so* lines and then under his guidance, I became just like him; women were to be used, never loved."

Between my shattered heart and my hangover, I've lost my appetite. "Am I just a sexual relationship for you?"

He doesn't meet my gaze. "It's what I wanted you to be."

I shove down the sting of his words. "But I'm more?"

"Yes."

"Do I mean something to you?"

His head turns and he locks me in the gaze of his broken soul. "I don't know what you mean to me, Emma, but you do mean something. I can't give you any more than that."

Megan's words trickle into my memory; *enjoy the ride or go all in and risk a broken heart. It could end up being the best thing that ever happened to you.* If I'm the first woman to mean something to Grayson since Danielle, then there's hope. I'm not willing to give up on him, not when he's giving me a crack to slip through. I want him with all of my heart and I know that now, forward is the only option.

"I'd like to finish breakfast together and then enjoy what you have planned."

Grayson stops me when I pick up my fork. "You deserve better than a cold waffle. I'd like to take you somewhere for a warm, satisfying meal."

A smile sneaks across my face. "I have no interest in arguing with that."

As we walk into the cafe, Grayson places his hand onto my back, giving me the first touch of affection I've received from him today. He asked me where I wanted to go and I said Laurel's Cafe. They have the best soups and sandwiches in town and my stomach could use the comfort food. Before we sit in the booth, his kiss on my head gives me as much relief as it does butterflies. That simple gesture shows me we're getting back to how we were before yesterday's fiasco.

"What should I get?" he asks me as he looks over the menu.

"Mmm, I think you'd like the roast beef and mashed potatoes."

He sets the menu back in its placeholder and winks. "Roast beef it is."

"I appreciate everything you did this morning; getting my bracelet fixed, going to my apartment and getting my things, and breakfast."

"I wanted you to wake up and have a good birthday."

I give him a reassuring smile. "You did good." I touch my fingers to my bracelet and rub my thumb over the stones. "I truly appreciate all of it."

"I know you do." His gaze studies my face and my cheeks warm. "The earrings look beautiful on you."

Grayson rises from his seat and I watch curiously as he moves to my side of the booth and joins me. With a finger, he brushes my hair off my shoulder, exposing my ear and neck.

"After seeing how upset you were last night, all I want to do is touch you." Like a butterfly kissing a flower, his lips graze my skin. With the added caress of his strong hand along my neck, I close my eyes, giving into the incredible sensation drifting over my shoulders. "I want you to stay the night with me, Emma. I need to be inside you. There's no better place."

Squeezing his thigh through his jeans, my body warms with arousal. "On one condition."

"What is it?"

I turn my head to see his curious stare. "You use the vibrator too."

He pulls his lip between his teeth and my nipples harden. His expression is priceless and I can't help grinning. I admit, Grayson has unleashed my inner kinky and there's no going back. When he goes to speak, he's interrupted by an older, round-faced waitress with a one dimple smile.

Smacking her gum, she asks, "What can I get you two lovebirds?"

"I'll take the grilled ham and cheese with the potato soup and a water."

Grayson rubs his brow, still smiling from cheek to cheek. "I'll take the roast beef and mashed potatoes and I'll have a water too."

When she winks, her lid shows off her dark eye shadow. "Coming right up," she says before disappearing into the back.

Grayson's thumb draws circles on my neck as his hand reaches between my legs. He leans close and whispers, "I promise to make you feel incredible."

Between the touch of his hand and the salacious thoughts running through my mind, my body is buzzing with need. "You always do."

He strokes my hair before he kisses my cheek.

The food arrives and Grayson's hand never leaves my thigh, rubbing me with his thumb each time I look at him. When the bill arrives, he leaves cash on the table and then slides out of the booth. "You ready for the next part of your birthday?"

I take his hand and exit the booth. I lean into him when he places his arm around me. "Very. I'm curious as to what you have planned."

On the drive to the mystery place, I text my mother and Megan. I let my mother know I'll call her later and thank her for the birthday wishes. I respond to

Megan's cute birthday Facebook post and she texts me seconds later.

With Grayson today?

Yes, he planned something special. He's not telling me what it is. Heading to it now.

Aww, that's romantic. Call me later when you get a chance, so we can plan to get together. I have a present to give my bestie. Happy Birthday! Love you!

Will do. Love you too!

Returning my phone to my purse, Grayson takes my hand in his and kisses my fingers. The usual flutter of emotion fills me and I watch him as he drives. With his blue and white flannel and dark jeans, he looks stylish, casual and sexy. He smiles when he catches me staring.

"I'm glad you chose to spend the day with me."

"Me too."

"Have you been to Glendale Park before?"

Turning into the entrance, I take notice of the large sign with the park name etched into the stone. With the park being on the edge of town it's a great place for people to walk the trails, have family picnics, or special events.

"Yeah, I've been here a time or two. I remember coming here once with my parents and flying kites when I was little."

"There's something special that happens every Saturday in the park."

Grayson pulls his car into a parking spot and my eyes widen at the sight in front of me. There's a booth with a canopy and next to it, a colorful red, orange, yellow, and white hot air balloon tethered to the ground. The operator is moving a lever, blowing flames, preparing the balloon for takeoff.

"Is this the surprise?"

His smile is wide in reaction to my excitement. "It is."

"Oh my God, Grayson, this is awesome! You're taking me on a hot air balloon ride!"

"Come on, Princess. Your carriage awaits you."

Dashing out of his car, I run to him and jump, wrapping my arms around his neck. "Thank you!"

His breath escapes him, and then he laughs and runs his hands over my hair and back. "This is the smile I hoped to see on your birthday. I had a feeling you'd love this."

Taking my hand in his, he leads me to the booth, gives his name and our ID's, then we're escorted to the balloon where he hoists me over the basket before joining me.

Marshall, an older man with a full beard and contagious smile, gives us the run down on the do-and-don'ts, then gives the ok to his assistant to release the ropes. They're pulled inside and then we're off.

Peering out at the landscape, I stand inside Grayson's arms and it feels perfect. His body is warm and his cologne is drifting in the breeze, a fragrance that's both masculine and tantalizing. For this time, it's just him and me up here without the problems of life below.

The way he's holding me, caressing my arm with his thumb, tells me what he struggles to say with words. I know he cares a lot for me to plan something like this, to take care of me last night, and ensure I have a great birthday. I can't expect a man who hasn't given his heart to a woman in fifteen years to suddenly give it willingly, without difficulty. I get it, he's a man who needs baby steps, and I'm willing to be patient. I have to be because I can't imagine a future without him.

Turning in his arms, I place my lips on his and thank him with all the emotion swimming through my body. His hand lowers to my ass and grips me tight against him. I feel him stretching against my thigh and he pulls back from our heated kiss.

The gentle touch of his hand grazes my jaw before thumbing my swollen lips. Staring at me with his penetrating blue-green eyes, I can see his fiery need beneath them. The desire between us is palpable. Our bodies arch toward one another, craving the contact. Forehead to forehead, his lips are a whispered breath from mine. "What are you doing to me?"

"It's what you're doing to me."

Warm lips greet me in a sensual embrace. The sweep of his tongue strokes across mine, teasing me like a wicked lure.

The operator clears his throat and Grayson pulls back, our breaths heavy. He drops his hand, the fire in his eyes fades away and our incredible moment is gone. With warm cheeks, I turn back to the horizon and Grayson rubs my shoulders as we look out at the sky.

It's a vision to be cherished. A view of the city and beyond that, the ocean as far as the eye can see. The blast of the fire behind us reminds me this view is on borrowed time, but it doesn't matter. It's a memory that will last forever.

CHAPTER 19

UMBLING THROUGH GRAYSON'S FRONT DOOR I giggle from the effects of that extra glass of wine during dinner. Grayson's mouth curves in a humored smile. I twirl into the living room, in my pretty black dress and fuck-me heels.

"Today has been amazing."

Closing the door behind us, he removes his jacket, still watching me curiously. The look in his eyes transitions to a lust-filled gaze as he admires me while I unzip the back of my dress.

"But it's not over yet. There's one thing left." Sliding my dress off my shoulders, I lower it down to my waist and glide it over my hips.

Grayson's eyes are locked on me, watching every movement.

I step out of the dress, only wearing the black heels. With cat-like precision, I move to where he stands.

Taking his tie in my hand, I loosen the knot, then remove it from his collar.

Grayson's eyes follow me and the tie as I spin it in my hand, give him a wink and head toward his room.

Before I reach the bedroom, Grayson has his arms around my waist and his lips to my neck, spreading wet kisses across my skin, creating a satisfying sensation all throughout my body.

Reaching the bed, I turn in his arms and unbutton his shirt. Pulling the fabric from his pants, I slide it off his muscled arms. My hands waste no time removing his belt and pants as his mouth crashes into mine, devouring my lips with aggressive need.

"There's no holding back tonight, Emma. I'm going to have you, all of you, every part of you. I want you needy and begging for my cock to be inside you."

My words brush across his lips. "I already want you, Grayson. I'm already there."

"No, Princess. Not even close."

Backed to his bed, I'm spread out before him, my heels against the mattress. Looking up, I see his erection, full and stretched tight. Desperate to taste it, I lick my lips. Grayson hisses and his cock jumps. Kneeling on the bed, he takes the tie from my hand. It's wrapped and knotted around my wrists, pulling them together above my head. Stretching my arms, he hooks the tie onto a tiny, black loop on the headboard. I glance up. *How the hell did I not notice that before?*

"At any point you want me to stop, Emma, just say so."

Anticipation spreads throughout my body, heating my core. "Less talking, Grayson, more doing."

The fire in his eyes burns brightly as he looks me over. "You're stunning, Emma. I obsess over every curve of your body."

He languidly strokes across my hip and down my thigh. Spreading my legs wider, he moves between them. Licking his fingers, he reaches down, massaging my clit. My body arches into his touch, eager for more.

"I can never get enough of your sweet pussy."

My head drops back as his tongue licks across my opening then dips inside my folds. With his one hand still rubbing my clit, my breath quickens and my body is aflame, burning with desire.

Grayson switches between sucks and flicks of his tongue, all the while his thumb circles my clit. His name seeps from my lips. My arms pull at the tie as the scorching heat between my legs ignites, my orgasm sending my body over the edge.

His weight leaves the bed and he stops at the dresser and removes the vibrator. Returning to the bed, the taste of me touches my lips as he kisses me deep. Pulling my bottom lip between his teeth, he reaches between my legs, sliding his fingers in and out. The unexpected touch of his wet fingers reaches farther down, to my very, tight hole. My body jerks back and he thumbs over my clit.

"Relax, Princess."

With a flick of his finger, the vibrator is turned on. Placing it on my clit, he moves it in circles. My body instantly relaxes and I spread my legs for him. His sensual gaze is steady on mine as he slides the vibrator into me. The intensity of the vibration reignites my arousal. Fingering my tiny hole, Grayson slides one digit in, gently moving in and out.

"Do you like the way this feels?"

I'm overwhelmed by the sensations of both his finger and vibrator working each hole, yet so turned on I don't want it to end.

"Yes," I breathe.

Another finger is added and I clench, then relax again as the vibrator is pressed just right, pushing my body toward another orgasm.

"Grayson, I need you. I need you inside me."

"I know you do. You're dripping wet for me."

Removing the vibrator, he flicks the button, turning it off, while still stretching and working my little hole.

Removing his fingers, his hands take hold of my legs and flip my body while the loop I'm bound to swivels, keeping me and the tie secured. Raising my ass, he spreads my legs and I feel his tip press to my opening. As soaked as I am, he slides right in and I let out a breath as he fills me, satisfying my desperate need for him.

With each thrust, I push back against him, slapping my ass to his pelvis. He holds me tight with one hand on my upper leg. A damp finger touches my little hole and then he slides it in. The sensations coursing through my body tip me over the edge. I come hard and fast, my body trembling uncontrollably.

Pulling out, Grayson touches his tip to my stretched hole. I bite my lip at the pinch I feel. Trailing tender kisses along my shoulder, he wraps his hand around my hip, caressing my clit, relaxing my body as he moves forward and back.

"Am I the first to have you like this?" His breath warms my ear as he continues to move in and out slowly, filling me as no other man has.

"Yes."

My hands drop as the tie is released from the swivel hook. Grayson's tender, affectionate kisses continue up my neck and shoulders, heightening the pleasure I'm already feeling.

"Will you let me come inside you?"

Feeling nothing but pleasure from each thrust now, I move my hips faster. "Yes. I want you to come inside me."

Twisting my hair in his hand, Grayson tugs. Gripping my hip with the other hand, he thrusts a little harder. A moan escapes my lips as my body tingles with a newly discovered arousal.

A growl escapes his chest and I feel him thicken. Bracing my hands on the headboard, each thrust draws a passionate cry from my lips.

"I want to hear you come, Princess."

"Grayson…don't stop."

His fingers reach for my clit, rubbing in circles as my orgasm builds, then explodes, pouring over his hand. Thrusting hard, he lets out a deep, satisfied moan as his own orgasm explodes.

My hair is freed from his grip and he takes hold of my hips as he slowly pulls out. Wrapping his arms around me, he lifts me, putting my back to his warm chest as he massages my breasts. "There's something very satisfying about being the only man to have been inside you like that."

Laying my head against his shoulder, residual pleasure lingers and trickles through my body. "You were right. That felt incredible."

His warm breath tickles my ear. "Now that I know you like it, I'm already looking forward to the next time I get to come inside your tight, little hole."

My fingers intertwine through his as he cups my breasts. "I can't even play coy. I'm looking forward to it too."

Evening stubble brushes across my cheek. "Promise me something."

"Anything."

"You won't let another man have what's mine."

If words could dance across a heart, they'd be prancing across mine. "Am I yours?" My breath is held, awaiting his answer.

"Yes, Princess, you are." Damp lips kiss my cheek and my heart stills. I'm safely cocooned in this moment, fully aware I own a piece of Grayson's heart, a piece not easily given, making me feel all the more special.

My moment of rapture is interrupted at the sound of his voice. "Let's get you into a bath. I don't want you to be sore."

Stepping off the bed, he takes my hand, leading me to the bathroom.

With dim lights and warm, soapy water filling the tub, he removes my heels and makes sure I'm settled in before joining me. Leaning back, I rest myself against his chest as he cups the water and releases it over my shoulders and chest.

"I've had an amazing birthday because of you."

"The weekend isn't over. Your birthday can continue tomorrow too."

Unease tickles my chest. "Megan wants to see me tomorrow. I'd like to spend some time with her too."

Tilting my head back, he dips my hair into the water and kisses my forehead. Lifting my head, he reaches for the shampoo. "So, I won't be seeing you tomorrow?" His disappointment is clear.

"Not necessarily. I can come over after I see Megan. I'm not sure what time that will be yet. I need to work out the details with her tomorrow morning."

"Will you be going out to a club or bar?" I can hear the tension in his voice.

"No, probably a mani and pedi, then dinner."

Strong hands massage the shampoo into my scalp and I purr with pleasure with each caring stroke.

"I'd like you back in my bed after you see Megan."

The wicked, little vixen in me enjoys challenging his commands. "And what are you willing to do to make that happen?"

A humored chuckle escapes him. "More like what I'll do if you're *not* in my bed."

Warmth rushes between my legs. "Oh, and what's that?"

With his hand gripping my hair, he pulls my head back, teasing me with a sensual tug. His lips brush along my ear. "I'll take you over my knee and spank your sweet ass."

I giggle as he places me back into the water to rinse my hair. "You think that's punishment? Sounds like a good time to me."

The corner of his mouth raises and he laughs. "I've turned a good girl into a very dirty one."

The warm water trickles down my chest as I raise myself and turn to face him, placing my hands around his neck. "I've always been a good girl, but with very wicked thoughts. You make me want to fulfill them."

Taking my hips in his hands, he slides me onto his erection. My breath catches and his brow raises as he grins with satisfaction. "Show me, Princess."

CHAPTER 20

EMMA

THE TOUCH OF GRAYSON'S HAND warms my shoulder and I turn away from the sunlit morning view to his handsome face. Reaching out, I take the coffee cup he's brought me and raise the reviving drink to my lips.

"Did you get a hold of Megan?" he asks, his eyes studying the city beyond his window.

"I did. I'm going to head home soon. She's meeting me there. What will you get into today?"

"I have several manuscripts from you and Rachel I need to look at and make offers on."

All it takes is to hear the sound of her name and irritation settles in my chest. "Did your meeting with her go well?"

Grayson's jaw flexes and I wonder the cause. "It went well. I'm going to get to work making a few calls. Stop in my office before you leave."

The swift change of subject seems abrupt and it causes discomfort to coil in my belly.

"Will do, Boss."

Glancing over his shoulder he winks at me. "That's right, Princess. Remember that."

I giggle behind my mug. Grayson stops, sets his mug on the top of the dresser and shifts his footing. His expression is playful, yet fierce—a warning.

"Oh shit!" I set the mug down on his book stand and take off for the bathroom.

With a few quick steps, I'm captured in his arms and giggling as he lifts me off my feet, carrying me to the bed and tossing me onto it. His sensual, dangerous gaze stares down at me as he lowers the zipper of his pants. "I think you need a lesson in obedience, Princess."

I nibble my lip as heat rushes to my core. "I think I do too."

A low hiss escapes him. "You're killing me with your needy pussy."

Slapping my bare legs together, I smirk as I reach my hand into my panties. "I can always take care of it myself."

Gripping my knees, he spreads my legs. "That's mine, Princess. All fucking mine."

SKILLED HANDS MASSAGE LOTION INTO my feet and my head falls back as a euphoric sensation sweeps over me. "Ah, this is Heaven."

Megan wiggles her freshly painted nails in my direction. The ceiling lights catch the glimmering sparkles and they shimmer with each movement of her fingers. "Is this not the best? I love how my nails turned out."

Tilting my head for a better view, I admire them. "They're gorgeous. I'm sure Jordan will like having them clawing at his back."

The curve of her mouth raises playfully. "He totally will."

"Things still going good?"

Placing her pretty hands back on her legs, she nods. "They are. Spent most of this week together. How about you and Grayson?"

"Amazing." I look into her big, brown eyes as hesitancy tightens my muscles. "I'm in love with him, Megs."

Her mouth contorts into a smirk. "I could've told you that. I could see it last week with the way you two looked at each other."

My brows pinch inward. "You think he loves me?"

"I do, but I don't think he's the kind of man to say it first."

My glorious foot rub comes to an end and the first foot is wrapped in a heated towel, warming my moisturized skin. "He's not. I'm scared to tell him."

"You shouldn't be scared to tell him how you feel about him."

"It's almost slipped out twice now and that worries me."

"I wouldn't let what happened with Derrick hold you back. If you're all in, then be all in. I mean he took you on a hot air balloon ride, bought you diamond and sapphire jewelry, gives you roses every day of the week, and hoards you all weekend, every weekend. The man adores you."

My body tingles with the overwhelming sense of adoration and affection from Megan's words. "He does adore me. He's said so himself, but I don't know Megs. He has issues with relationships. I don't want to scare him off."

"What do you mean? You told me he's thirty-six. What relationship issues does he have?"

As my toenails are polished, I share Grayson's past and our conversation at his kitchen table.

Megan angles her head, her expression empathetic. "I think the guy loves you but doesn't know how to say it since he hasn't felt it in years."

Glancing down, I admire my teal colored toenails. "You think so?"

"I do. I don't think he knows how to express it verbally, but his actions are speaking loud and clear."

"I was thinking of surprising him and getting some new sexy lingerie while we're out. What do you think?"

A playful smirk lifts her lips. "I think that's a brilliant idea. I'll help you pick out something that will make his hard-on tear through his pants."

Both pedicure technicians glance up at Megs, and we all laugh.

Inside the lingerie store, the lights are bright and the scent of rose petals lingers in the air. Megs is a few racks over, gathering even more lacy and strappy items to add to her collection. Holding a few pieces in my left hand, I sift through a rack with my free hand. Pursing my lips, I giggle when I come across a matching set; black lace camisole top and crotchless panties. Taking a pair, in both red and black, I nod to Megs. "I'm ready to try on a few things."

"Me too."

Following me closely, we enter the dressing room and wait for the attendant to count our items and unlock the doors for us. I go right for the crotchless outfit first. With the black one on and everything in place, I grab my phone and fidget in front of the mirror until I have an acceptable shot I can call sexy. Just when I go to click, my heel slips and my leg drops, slamming me into the mirror. "Ouch!"

"What are you doing in there?" Megs asks amid my grumbling and shoulder rubbing.

"Um...taking a picture with the crotchless panties on. I'm asking Grayson if he likes the red or black."

"Oh my God, you're ridiculous. Let me know what he says."

Laughing, I set up for another shot. Getting it just right this time, I hit send.

A few minutes later, as I'm slipping into a negligee, my phone dings. I pick it up and read the text. "Oh shit! That's hot!"

"What did he say?

"He sent me a video clip."

"Oh!"

"Yeah," I mumble as I replay the video of Grayson stroking his erection.

My phone dings again and a new message pops up, interrupting the sexy video that's making me wet watching it.

You have me thinking how much I want to slip between the fabric. I want you to buy both, Princess. Wear the black tonight.

Will do ;) Hot video btw

Like that?

Fuck yes!

The sooner you're back, the sooner you can have it inside you.

I'll eat fast. ;)

Good. All I can think about now is how much I want to fuck you wearing those crotchless panties.

Those are good thoughts to have.

Hurry up, Princess. I want you.

Knuckles tap on the fitting room door and I jump.

"Are you still sexting him? I'm done trying on."

Sliding the phone into my purse, I hurry to change. "I'm done too."

"Make sure you didn't leave any stains from your cumtastic party in there."

"Megs!" She laughs, I roll my eyes.

"Hey, you're the one sexting and videogramming your vagina while trying on lingerie, which was a great idea by the way. I'm totally sexting Jordan pics when I get home."

Opening the door, I have no doubt my heated cheeks are rosy pink. Megs winks and waves at the lingerie in my hand. "Let me see what you chose."

Raising the lingerie, I show off each piece and she does the same. A quick walk to the register and we're checking out.

With our pink bags in hand, Megs puts her arm through mine. "Ready for dinner, birthday girl? I'm starving."

"As long as there's birthday cake."

Still buzzed from the Mojitos I drank, I double-check that I have everything in my bag before heading out my apartment door to the cab that's waiting. Sure that I have what I need, I put the strap over my shoulder, locking the door behind me.

Outside, the cool breeze gives my vagina a brisk wake-up call and I slap my thighs closer together as I walk the few remaining feet to the cab. With butterflies in my belly, I hop in and give the cabbie directions to Grayson's condo.

I'm practically dancing in my heels by the time the elevator reaches his floor. I knock on his door, but he doesn't answer. Disappointment fills me before I reach for the knob; the door opens, he left it unlocked for me.

Entering his condo, I see a glass of white wine waiting on the kitchen counter for me. Taking the glass, I head to his bedroom. Passing his office, I look inside to check if he's there. Seeing an empty office, I take a sip of the wine and continue on. Inside his room, I can hear the shower running. I drop my bag by the bed and move to the window to admire the moonlit sky over the city.

The shower turns off and my stomach flutters with excitement. Hearing movement behind me, I glance over my shoulder to see him in the doorway of the bathroom with a towel wrapped around his shoulders, using an end of it to dry his hair. His gaze settles on me and he smiles. He tosses the towel, leaving it in the bathroom.

Watching him walk toward me, his muscles taut

and his erection growing, dampens my core. Approaching my back, his fingers graze mine as he takes the wine glass from my hand and sets it on the bookstand.

Moving his hands along the fabric of my dress, his voice is husky when he asks, "Did you wear them?" Placing his hands on the hem of my dress and with achingly slow movements, he raises it up my thighs.

I bite back my grin. "I did."

His erection presses into my cheeks. "Good girl."

Intertwining his fingers with mine, he raises them and places my hands against the window as his lips leave a trail of sensuous kisses along my ear and down my neck.

A whimper escapes me and he presses harder into my ass. "Did you miss me today?"

"So much."

Caressing down my arms, his hands find my breasts and massage them. With my nipples pressing through my camisole and dress, he gives attention to each, hardening them and drawing out my insatiable desire.

"Did you miss having my cock inside you?" Abandoning my breasts, one hand takes hold of my hip and thumbs the strap of my underwear.

"Yes."

Sliding his tip between my legs, he wets it with the slick heat of my arousal. "Do you want it now, Princess?"

"Yes, I want you deep inside me."

Gripping my hip tight, he enters me, filling me

completely. Ecstasy seizes my body and I eagerly move my ass against him. With a firm hold on my hip, the other hand wraps around me, squeezing my breast as our bodies slap together and my palms leave sex driven smudges on his window.

My satisfied moans are a chorus paired with the sounds of our bodies coming together. Taking my desire to its highest point, my body trembles through an orgasm. I feel him thicken and hear a sated breath escape him as he reaches his own climax.

Kissing my shoulder tenderly, he caresses up my arms. Taking my hands in his, he rests his cheek against mine. "Why do you feel better than any woman I've ever been with?"

With my heart heavy with emotion, I nuzzle closer. "Because you love me."

My eyes widen hearing the sobering comment that slipped from my lips. *Did I seriously just say that?*

The knot tightening in my gut expands at his silence. He pulls out of me and the sudden detachment leaves me feeling isolated and eager for his touch again.

"Let's get cleaned up." His tone lacks all the emotion it had moments ago.

My throat feels tight, as though something is constricting it. Panic surges through me. Tensing, I lower my dress. "All right if I take a shower?"

"Whatever you need."

Turning to look at him, I see he's already moved away, heading to the bathroom. I swallow the lump in my throat and follow him. Starting the shower, he kisses my cheek before walking away. His kiss is quick, emotionless, and it scares me.

"Grayson."

He turns back, my voice drawing his attention.

"I didn't mean to—"

He smiles and I know it's forced. "Enjoy your shower, Emma," he cuts me off and is gone out the door in seconds.

With tears burning my eyes, I undress and step into the warm, soothing water. It keeps the full-on tears from shedding. As I douse my loofa with my soap and scrub my body, I analyze every detail of Grayson's response and what he's potentially thinking and how he might react to what I said.

I fight back the tears trying to escape when I realize I could be wrong. He may not love me like I thought.

With the towel wrapped around me, I open the door to his room. Grayson isn't there and I'm even more worried as I put on my new negligee and dry my hair. Hoping to find him, I search his condo, checking his office first. He's not there either. The spare bedroom is pointless, but I check anyway. A walk through the living room and kitchen proves he's left the condo.

Unsure of what to do, I retrieve the wine glass from his room and pour a fresh glass in the kitchen. Calling his phone, it goes straight to voicemail. I pour another glass as the clock ticks by and Grayson is still a no-show.

An hour later, sleep pulling at my eyelids, I tuck

myself into his blankets, breathing in the lingering scent of his cologne. Tears trickle down my cheeks as I wonder if I'll be sleeping in his bed alone all night or if maybe I should go home.

HEARING MOVEMENT IN THE CONDO startles me awake. I glance at the clock on the nightstand. Blue lights display 1:36 a.m. Grayson enters his room, moving with heavy steps and no attempt to be quiet. Shifting for a better view of him, he glances at me. His eyes narrow. Clearly, he's surprised to see me. Undressing down to his gorgeous naked frame, he crawls into the bed, over me.

My thoughts dart between wondering where he's been, what he's been doing, why he left, yet my body tingles, responding to his tender expression. Holding himself up, he stares down at me with glossy eyes and heavy lids. The scent of scotch is distinct on his breath. Caressing my cheek with his hand, he studies my face. "Do you love me?"

Tension tightens in my chest. *It's now or never, Emma.* "Yes, I'm in love with you."

His silence is a weight pressing down on my body,

threatening to crush me. Staring at me, his eyes roaming my face, he kisses my lips, slowly, sensually, taking me by surprise. He removes the sheet from between us and raises my negligee to my waist.

Never taking his lips from mine, he reaches under the silky fabric, finding my breast and kneading it as he slides between my legs and presses his erection into me. Desire ripples through my body and eclipses all emotions jumbling my mind. Everything goes blank as heat and need fill me. With each passionate thrust, he loves my body with his.

For the first time, he makes love to me and I know in this moment, Grayson Cole owns my heart.

CHAPTER 21

GRAYSON

'VE READ OVER THE SAME damn paragraph on my computer screen for the last twenty minutes. I have no idea what it says because my thoughts are elsewhere. This weekend with Emma was one of the most enjoyable weekends I've ever had, probably, the most enjoyable. Yet, it took her saying four words to turn my head into a shit storm. I bolted like a wild animal and drowned my confusion in whiskey rather than face her and admit any sort of feelings.

No doubt, adding to her confusion, I got piss-ass drunk, came home and had sex with her. When I woke from what little sleep I had, I looked over at her sleeping peacefully. She'd had an incredible birthday weekend and the last thing I wanted was for her to wake up and look at me with worry or confusion in her eyes. Like a bad habit, I left her again. It's better that way. I need the time to think.

My office phone rings and I appreciate the distraction.

"Hello, Son."

Just what I fucking need.

"Arnold."

"Have you had enough time to bury your dick in that girl's pussy and get over the disagreement we had Friday night?"

As if I'm not tense enough. "Tell me a good reason not to hang up."

"It doesn't matter if you're still angry with me. We have business that needs to be completed. I emailed you several files. You'll need to read over them and provide your signature. Now, in regards to our disagreement and this girl, you know very well I did what I did because I care about you. Getting feelings involved will only get you fucked over, you know I'm right. That whore you loved in college wasn't the only one to prove me right. You've had other women that were only interested in riding your cock and draining your bank account. Tell me I'm wrong. This girl, she isn't special. She isn't different from the others. She's new. Given time, she'll do what they all do."

My jaw's so tight, my teeth are painfully grinding together. A dull ache is forming in my hand gripping the phone. "We have a type, Arnold. We seek out beautiful, independent women who only want sex and money from us. Emma doesn't give a damn about money or what it can get her. She's in love with me."

Arnold snickers. "You're being a fool. She loves

what you can offer her. I see her wearing the diamonds you bought her, and no doubt, you spared no expense. But what has she done for you, Son? Love is an illusion. Do you truly want the picket fence, two-and-a-half kids, the damn dog, all to fall hopelessly in love and then have it ripped away from you? Get your head together and end things, *now*. The girl is your employee for fuck sake. She's young with many opportunities awaiting her. You think she'll stick around when they come along?"

The Atlanta job comes to mind and the lump in my throat drops to my stomach. "I have work to do. I'll look over the files and get back to you."

"The sooner you end things with her, the better."

I disconnect without a goodbye. Leaning back in my chair, I loosen my suit jacket and look out the window to the city beyond it, trying to calm my agitation. My gaze shifts to the clock on my monitor. Emma will be arriving any moment and that realization adds to my unease.

—EMMA—

As soon as I enter my office, the first thing I notice is there's no rose. Disappointment filters in, adding to my concern. After all that happened the night before and waking up to Grayson being gone, I'm worried that the missing rose might mean something. We haven't had a chance to talk and I'm anxious to see him.

I drop my purse by my desk and turn on my computer. As I pass Claire's office I wave but don't stop to chat. I head straight to Grayson's office. The glass is un-shaded and I can see him standing with his arm above his head, resting on the window, looking at the city. The side profile of his face reveals he's deep in thought. Jittery nerves come alive as I reach for the door knob. His attention remains out the window as I enter.

"Grayson."

He lowers his head before looking at me. "Morning Emma. What can I do for you?"

His melancholy voice and all-business demeanor startle me. "You were gone when I woke up. I was anxious to see you this morning."

Giving me a half-smile, he doesn't seem interested in coming any closer.

"I had some work I needed to start. I apologize for leaving last night without an explanation."

Tension builds as I slowly step closer, desperate for contact. "Can I have an explanation now?"

With his hands in his pockets, he stares at me and I try to read the emotion in his eyes, but he's expressionless, poker-faced.

"It's not the best time for us to have this discussion, Emma. We can talk after work."

His words and actions tear away at my heart. I'm confused, worried, and all I want to do is kiss him and be comforted by his touch. Before the tears start falling, I nod and show my own poker-face.

"All right, we'll talk later."

Walking out of his office, I see Claire in the lunchroom making a cup of coffee. With my emotions running rampant, I join her, needing to vent. I stand there for several moments gathering my composure before pouring my own cup.

Claire nudges my arm with her elbow. "Something's totally up with you, but I have something that might make you feel better. I got you a present!" she singsongs.

Raising my head, I meet her gaze. "That's so sweet of you. Thank you."

"Of course. Did you have a good weekend? I assumed you spent it with Grayson."

The sound of his name tugs at my heart and threatens tears.

"Oh no, something going on between you two?"

"I think so, but I don't know what. He won't talk to me and left this morning before I woke up."

Her lip juts out below her empathetic gaze. "I'm sorry, Em. Maybe he's trying to sort through whatever is going on with him."

The warm liquid does nothing to soothe my tension and my shoulders drop. "I think that's exactly what's going on. I'm scared of the outcome."

My attention drifts to Rachel in her purple dress

and high heels as she saunters into the lunchroom and grabs the coffee carafe.

She takes one glance at me and smirks. "Trouble in paradise?"

"Fuck off," I snap.

She snickers. "Guess so. Did Grayson finally get around to telling you he recommended me for the Branch Agent position in Atlanta? I'd be pissed too if I was in your shoes. Guess your boyfriend thought I was a better fit. Even if he has poor taste in who he fucks, at least he can recognize talent." With a smug expression, she takes a sip of her coffee, then saunters out of the lunchroom.

My attention whips to Claire. "What is she talking about? What job in Atlanta?"

Claire sets her mug on the counter, her expression revealing the same distress as mine. "She's such a bitch. I heard a rumor that Schmidt and Costello might be opening a new branch in Atlanta. That has to be what she's talking about."

My anger and confusion escalate. I set the mug down as my hands tremble. "I need to call Headquarters and find out what's going on. I'll catch up with you later."

Returning to my office, I sift through my list of numbers in my contact list. Finding the right one, I call Mr. Johnston.

"Schmidt and Costello. Mr. Johnston speaking."

"Mr. Johnston it's Emma Williams from the Florida branch. How are you?"

Papers rustle in the background, then silence. "I'm good. Thank you for asking. What can I do for you, Miss Williams?"

"I'm calling to learn more about the position in Atlanta. I hear you might be opening a branch there."

"I can confirm we are." His tone shifts. "I'm surprised this news hasn't been given to you already."

Frustration coils in my chest. "I'm just as surprised as you are."

"I was also surprised when you didn't apply for the position. This explains why. The announcement closed Friday, but if you're interested and can complete the application today, I'll squeeze you in."

"I appreciate that very much, Mr. Johnston. I am interested and I can have it completed today. Not a problem."

"Great. I'll send you the application link via email. You'll need Mr. Cole to approve it before it can officially be submitted."

Tension spreads over my shoulders. "I'll take care of that. Thank you, Mr. Johnston."

We disconnect and I focus on taking calm breaths. Standing from my chair, I pace to the window and back, then decide to face the issue head on. I stomp my way to Grayson's office and even though the windows are shaded, I open the door and enter. Grayson is on the office phone, his brows pinched inward.

"I understand, Mr. Johnston. Thank you for the call."

Shit. No doubt he knows his secret is blown.

Grayson hangs up and leans back in his chair, waiting for me to say what I clearly stormed into his office for.

"The meeting with Rachel was to tell her about the job opportunity in Atlanta, wasn't it? *Why* didn't you tell me about it?"

He adjusts his jacket, his expression blank. "I was being selfish. I didn't want you to take it."

"You have no right to make that kind of decision for me! How could you do that? If I hadn't called Mr. Johnston just now, I would have missed the opportunity!"

"You're right. I don't have that right, I shouldn't have hidden the job from you. I'll approve the request when you're done completing the application."

Looking at me silently, he gives me nothing else, no emotion, no apology, no explanation for last night, and my anger turns to rage.

"I told you I loved you last night and that scares you, and now you're shutting me out! How is it you can go through the trouble of keeping me from a job promotion, but you can't even tell me how you feel about me?"

Grayson flexes his jaw, the first sign of emotion I've seen today. "You want to take this job, perhaps you don't love me as much as you think you do."

My arms fold across my chest. "How the hell does wanting to better my career mean I don't love you?"

"We're both adults, Emma. We both know a long-distance relationship isn't practical. What we have has been great, but being your Boss, I never should've let things get as far as they have. You deserve that job. Don't let whatever this is—" he points to me and him "—get in the way."

"*Whatever this is*? What the hell does that mean? Because my understanding is that we're in a relationship, re-lat-ion-ship, Grayson, that means two people care and love one another. I know you feel the same way about me as I do about you, but you're too damn proud and scared to admit it!"

"Emma, I'm not scared or too proud."

"Then say it, Grayson. Tell me how you feel about me. Or tell me you don't love me! Either way, I'll at least know what you feel for me!"

Rubbing the nape of his neck, Grayson tries to relieve the tension I'm sure he's feeling. "Emma, this conversation should wait until after work. This isn't the place for us to be arguing."

"Bullshit! That's another cop out. You're avoiding me and your feelings." My heels click across the floor as I leave. Stopping with my hand on the door, I turn to face him. "You told me once that when someone hurts you, you have the choice to either let it weaken or strengthen you. You didn't let your heart break strengthen you. It's weakened you, Grayson, to the point you refuse to let someone in and love them."

Silence. Shifting his gaze to the window, he makes no effort to stop me from leaving. I walk out with tears pooling in my eyes. Back in my office, I close the door and pull up the email with the application link. I wasn't sure I truly wanted to apply to this job, until that conversation. Now I'm sure—applying is the right choice.

HEARING MEGS FAMILIAR KNOCKING, I turn down the music I'm drunkenly dancing to. I open the door and her expression contorts as she raises on her toes and looks around my apartment behind me. "What the hell are you doing? And why are you in pajamas and boots dancing to Nancy Sinatra's These Boots are Made for Walking?"

Glancing down at my boots, I turn my ankles for her to admire them. "Claire got them for my birthday and I'm purging things I don't need. I applied for a job in Atlanta today and I have a damn good chance of getting it."

Megs pushes the door wider and enters, carrying a restaurant bag. After setting it on the counter, she sheds her jacket, tossing it on the couch. Leaning against the back of it, she crosses her arms. "Start explaining. Yesterday you're in love with Grayson and today you're taking a job in Atlanta. What happened?"

The scent of Thai food draws me to the bag and I

rummage through it, pulling out containers one at a time, ignoring her disappointed expression. "I told him I loved him, Megs, and he bolted. Today I found out he withheld a job opportunity from me because *he selfishly didn't want me to leave*. I called him out on everything. He told me to apply and that he never should have let things get as far as they did."

She approaches and I turn to look at her as she outstretches her arms. "I'm so sorry, Em."

I hug her quickly, pulling away before the tears escape. "I'm not letting it tear me down. I swore to myself that Derrick would be the last man to hurt me. I need to face Grayson and my relationship for what it was—an office fling."

Resting her hand on my arm, the affectionate movement of her thumb along my skin tugs at the tears threatening to fall from my eyes.

"I don't think it was a fling for either of you."

Turning away from her sad eyes, I begin opening the containers. My heart splinters and the pain seeps out. I take a deep breath and shove the pain away. "You're right. It wasn't for me. I wanted more, but we don't always get what we want."

Megs' curls swing when she reaches for her own container and chopsticks. "Are you sure it's over? Maybe he needs time to process how he feels."

With our containers in hand, we move to the couch. "Considering at the end of the work day he sent me an email saying he approved my application and wishes me the best of luck in my career pursuits, I'd say it's pretty clear how he feels."

Stopping mid-bite, she angles her head, frowning. "I didn't think Grayson was a dick, but he's quickly changing my mind."

"You and me both, but I don't want to talk about it. I drank half a bottle of wine to forget and I'd like to continue my plan, focusing on other, better things in my life."

"You really want to take this job?"

Not wanting to see the disappointment in her eyes, I keep my attention on my food. "I do. The promotion is a great opportunity. I'm ready for it."

"But you'll be moving to Atlanta...away from me."

Her melancholy tone tears at my already fragile emotions. Dropping my shoulders, I struggle to gain the courage to meet her gaze. "I know, but I'll only be a five-and-a-half hour drive or an hour flight away. We can still get together on the weekends. Plus, it's an excuse to have weekend sleepovers."

"I don't like it. I won't be able to pick up carryout and come over whenever I want to anymore. I won't be able to steal your shoes when I need a quick, sexy pair."

"You can have any pick of the litter," I quip, trying to extinguish the sorrow filling the air between us.

She rolls her eyes and smiles. "If you're leaving me, I'm taking more than one pair."

Chuckling, the laughter lifts some of the heavy weight of my emotions.

CHAPTER 22

EMMA

*I*T'S BEEN THREE DAYS AND Grayson has done everything he can to avoid me, and truthfully, I'm ok with it. I've been wanting to avoid him too. The two times we've crossed paths in the lobby, my whole body grew tense with a combination of anger and heartbreak. With his usual poker-face, he barely makes eye contact and continues on to where he's headed. It's better that we don't speak because I don't have anything appropriate to say to him. He is still my Boss, and I need to respect that, even if I want to throat punch him.

Everyone in the office can sense the tension between us. Claire says the office environment has become depressing since our break-up. To add to my already overwhelming emotions, Rachel discovered I applied for the position in Atlanta and nearly blew a gasket. Claire had to step in and threaten to write her up when Rachel barged into my office declaring that the only reason I applied was because I want to prove I'm better than her or some such bullshit.

Now I'm five minutes away from my interview, nervous as hell. Not because of the interview itself, but because this means I'm definitely going through with it and putting myself one step closer to uprooting my whole life.

I jolt when my office phone rings, then reach for it before pressing the speaker button, setting the receiver back down. On the other end is Mr. Johnston, and two other head honchos from Headquarters.

"Miss Williams, are you ready for your interview?" Mr. Johnston asks.

"I am."

"Wonderful. Let's begin."

Forty-seven minutes later, I take a relieved breath after ending the call. It was a brutal interview, but I'm confident I nailed it. They said they'd have an answer by Monday. It's unusually fast, and I wonder if they already know who they want to hire. If it's not me, I feel my worst nightmare coming to fruition. I know I'll begin looking for jobs elsewhere because I can't continue to see Grayson every damn day, feeling the way I do, when I know he doesn't feel the same.

Glancing at the clock, I see it's close to lunchtime. Grabbing my purse, I head to Claire's office. I could use a drink during lunch to settle my heightened nerves right about now. As I open my door and step out, I see Grayson and Rachel walking through the lobby like they're going to lunch together. Tears sting my eyes and anger surges up through my stomach and into my chest. I can feel my face getting hot and my fists clench. Grayson cuts off their conversation and heads right toward me.

Retreating to my office, he follows. As soon as the door closes, I attack.

"Fucking her now too? One office fling wasn't enough? Don't worry Grayson, you made the right choice—" I point toward where I last saw Rachel "— that one won't get attached."

Grayson's nostrils flare. "I'm not fucking Rachel. Take a breath, Emma. We need to talk."

"*Now*? You haven't spoken to me in *days* and now all the sudden, you want to talk after I caught you about to leave with Rachel?"

"*She* is going to lunch. I had no intention of joining her. We were discussing business."

Staring into his beautiful blue-green eyes feels like claws shredding my heart to pieces. I love this man, and after everything we shared, having him stand here like we're just a Boss and employee is killing me. It takes everything in me to keep my tears at bay. "I can't have this talk. I'm not ready to hear how you're sorry, that you cared for me, but it was never going to work. I've heard it before, and I can't take hearing it from you."

Bolting out my office, I don't bother finding Claire. I want to get as far away from him, as quickly as I can.

CHAPTER 23

GRAYSON

$\mathcal{I}$'M LEANING BACK IN MY office chair contemplating my decisions, as I've done every damn day this week, when Emma walks into the lobby. Her long, tight ponytail, knee-length black skirt, and stilettos stiffen my cock as I think back on the last time she wore that thigh-hugging skirt. She moaned repeatedly as her ass slid across my desk and my dick swelled inside her tight pussy.

Even though I don't want to admit it to myself, I know the discomfort I'm feeling is because I miss her. I miss leaving roses on her desk every morning and the smile she'd have when she walked into my office with it. I miss being inside her and the way she'd give herself over to me, losing herself to my touch and her desperate need for me and me alone. But it doesn't matter. I received the call first thing this morning. She's been chosen for the Atlanta job. As soon as she opens her email she'll discover it herself.

Running my hand along the stubble on my jaw, I watch her office door she entered minutes ago. As if on cue, she opens it, glances my direction and scurries to Claire's office. No doubt she's sharing the news of her promotion. I don't need to ask to know she'll accept it.

Our time together was always limited and deep down I knew that, but being with Emma brought a satisfaction into my life that I haven't experienced in over ten years. Selfishly, I wanted to keep her close so that I could continue to indulge in her affections, but just as I expected, she chose the job over me. I know she thinks she loves me, but Arnold is right—it's an illusion. She'll move to the new job and it won't be long before she catches the attention of another man. It won't be long before she's giving him her body and her love.

I pound my desk as anger surges through me. "Damn it!"

The son-of-a-bitch was right. It's better that I ended things before my feelings got more involved.

In the corner of my eye, I catch her movement coming out of Claire's office. Hesitantly, she approaches mine. As she enters, her expression is a mix of emotions I can't fully read.

Awkwardly fidgeting, as if unsure how to approach me or the subject she wants to discuss, she finally blurts it out. "As you know, I've been offered the position in Atlanta. Things are moving fast with the opening of the branch. They want me to fly there tomorrow to help with interviews and make hiring decisions. The full move will happen in three weeks. They're going to pay for a temporary apartment for thirty days, until I can find a place of my own."

The news stings, but I manage to force a smile. "Congratulations, Emma. You deserve the job. I imagine you'll take your client list with you?"

"Yes, anyone who isn't under contract with you, I'll be taking with me."

"Be sure to transfer all other duties to Rachel and Lisa for a smooth transition." The sound of those words escaping my mouth coil my stomach and I quickly shove down the unfamiliar sensation coursing through me.

"Of course. I'll try to make the transition as smooth as possible."

"I have no doubt you will. Anything else I can do for you?"

Her eyes darken and there's one emotion suddenly clear—anger.

"No, Grayson, there's nothing else you can do for me."

BEYOND MY WINDOW, THE MOON is hidden behind dark, dreary clouds. The sound of repeated tings hit the glass as the rain comes down, drowning the city under a blanket of water. The weather outside mocks my own misery, a reflection of my internal turmoil. Lifting the scotch to my lips, I use the alcohol to drown the memories of Emma's tear-filled eyes as she left my office this morning. My inability to commit has wounded her to the point she now hates me. Maybe it's better this way. She deserves better than me, a man who can't bring himself to trust another enough to love or be loved. She was right when she said I let Danielle's betrayal keep me from letting anyone else in.

Knocking at my door pulls me from my thoughts. I place my empty glass on the kitchen counter on my way to answer. Standing on the other side is Emma, soaking wet, hair drenched. Her eyes roam over me, still in my suit pants, my dress shirt unbuttoned and open. She steps forward and I take a step back, letting her in. Her glossy eyes and the scent of wine suggests she's had several drinks, too.

I instinctively raise my hand and brush a damp strand of hair away from her beautiful face. "What are you doing here?"

"I'm leaving tomorrow and I...I needed to see you, Grayson. Can we...for one night, forget everything that's happened between us? Can you touch me like you used to?"

My cock aches with the need to have her, to feel the release and freedom her body brings. Running my thumb along her bottom lip, her eyes close, her mouth slightly parts. With erotic sensuality, she sucks the tip of my finger between her lips. With my cock stretched tight and my desire to have her taking control, I remove my thumb and look into her alluring eyes. My voice catches in my throat as the emotion I see in her eyes takes hold of me. "Yes, Princess. I can."

Cupping my face, her lips crash into mine as I palm her ass cheeks and lift her, holding her tightly against my erection. Kicking the front door closed, I carry her to my room, never taking my lips from hers. Tearing at the fabric keeping us apart, we strip one another, landing in a needy, breathless heap on the mattress.

The warmth between her legs taunts me and I rush to fill it, to be inside her needy pussy, to have her moaning my name as I bring us both to orgasm. My lips burn kisses across her skin as her scorching heat surrounds me, consuming my breath. Intertwining our fingers, I thrust deep and hard, claiming her body.

LOOKING UP BETWEEN TIRED EYES, I see the clock says six a.m. My arm is still stretched out to where Emma's body laid next to me throughout the night. Unaware she left while I was sleeping, her absence is now felt by the void forming in my chest. Reaching for my phone I start a text, delete it, then toss the phone onto the bed. If she wanted to talk, she would have stuck around.

Her jasmine scent lingers in my bed, and I realize what last night was; it was closure, goodbye sex, and as incredible as it felt to have her beneath me, I need to remember she's leaving in three weeks. I got exactly what I started out to get—all of her, and she gave her love willingly. I refused to accept that love and now I'm getting what I deserve—loneliness and the feeling of desertion.

Maybe if I'd told her about the job and told her I wanted her to stay, perhaps she never would have applied in the first place. Maybe she'd be lying in my bed now, smiling up at me, ready to give me more of that love, willing to commit her heart and body to me and only me. Instead, I let my selfish pride get in the way. Now, I have no one to blame but myself for this gut-wrenching feeling.

Moving with quick steps, I search for clean clothes. I don't know why the hell I think this is a good idea, but I need to see her before she leaves. I need to fix everything I've destroyed.

WALKING INTO THE AIRPORT, I purchase a ticket to Atlanta without a second thought, search for a monitor, then scan the departing flights and their departure gates. Seeing the one I need, I walk briskly to the C4 gate where Emma will be. My heart rate speeds up as I near. I'm anxious to see her and worried she won't be happy to see me. Waiting to get through security, I search for her. She's nowhere to be found and this line is far too long. Taking out my phone, I call her. It goes straight to voicemail. *Damn it.*

With no choice, but to wait in line, I stand with arms crossed and my patience wearing thin as the process of getting travelers through moves painfully slow.

Twenty minutes later, I'm given the okay by the airport security employee, then nearly jog to find Emma's gate. Another two sections and I see her dark hair and stunning face in the distance. She's standing in line next to a young, good-looking man, her smile wide. They're talking, their phones raised as if exchanging numbers. The sight brings me to a dead stop. *This* is exactly why my idea to come for her was a mistake.

It's a decision I suddenly regret making. I was right. She's young and beautiful. It's only a matter of time before I'm just a memory—a memory of a flawed man who rejected her. I quickly turn before she sees me.

With heavy footed steps, I shove down the anger and frustration, making my way to the exit.

"Grayson!"

Her voice stalls me. I turn to see her eyes wide, her expression revealing her shock. She left the boarding line to catch me.

"What are you doing here?" she asks, her tone full of surprise.

My eyes dart to the young man watching her from the boarding line, then back to her. "Nothing, it was a mistake to come."

"Grayson, wait." Her hand reaches for mine, stopping me from leaving.

The feel of her soft hand stirs my emotions and makes what I'm about to say painfully difficult. With my eyes set on hers, I shut down my emotions, giving her the all-business tone. "*You* were a mistake. Last night was a mistake. You made the right decision taking this job." Tears show in her eyes and I force away the pain it causes me.

She shakes her head. "I don't believe you. That's not what you came here to tell me. We promised not to lie to each other. You're lying to me now."

"You lied too, Emma. You told me you loved me, then you took this job as if I meant nothing to you."

Her eyes narrow, but not entirely with anger, but confusion, too. "I took the job only because you don't want me. I no longer have a reason to stay. I can't take seeing you every day, desperate for your touch, longing for you to love me the way I love you. I have no choice but to move on. I won't let another man break me."

Taking her hands in mine, I affectionately rub my thumbs over them as I look into her sad eyes. The pain I see in them, it's all because of me. I did this to her. I did this to us. "I never wanted to break you or hurt you. I'm the one who's broken. I didn't realize what you meant to me until you made me face the thought of never having you in my arms again—" I lean my head against hers as the tears trickle down her cheeks "—of never seeing your beautiful smile every time you walk into the room, never hearing you moan from my touch. I've been selfish, Emma, too selfish and prideful to admit what you mean to me. Can you forgive me?"

Last call for boarding flight 422 to Atlanta. The airport attendants voice echoes around us, tearing through our conversation.

Emma raises her head and wipes away her tears. "I have to go, Grayson. I wish you would have told me this sooner. I'm sorry I have to leave. I'll call you when I get to Atlanta."

Her hand breaks away and I watch her back until she gathers her luggage bag and disappears into the boarding hall. Seeing her leave tears away at my ego, humbling me in a way I never thought possible.

The ride back to my condo is too long, giving me far too much time to think. What if it's too late? What if after all I've done to her, she's ready to move on? What if I've destroyed the best thing that's ever happened to me?

Back at the condo, I shower and get dressed for work, ready for a needed distraction to keep my mind off Emma until I can see her again. Next time, I'll fight harder. I'll do whatever it takes to get her to stay. I have to learn to trust her like she so willingly trusted me. I have to stop assuming the worst and start believing in what is possible between us.

I'm about to leave the condo when my phone rings in my pocket, it's Claire.

I try to make out what she's saying in between her sobs. "Turn...on...the TV."

I rush to the remote and turn to the news. My knees give out beneath me and I fall onto the couch. The words rush across my screen in bold letters; *FLIGHT 422 TO ATLANTA CRASHED EARLY THIS MORNING. 23 CONFIRMED DEAD. UPDATES TO FOLLOW.*

With trembling hands, I dial Emma's phone. "Pick up, Princess. *Please* pick up."

Her phone goes straight to voicemail and fear seizes me. All this time I took for granted what I had right in front of me, and now I might have lost her completely.

"Emma, don't be gone. *Please,* answer your phone." I call again and it cuts to voicemail.

I immediately dial Claire back as panic surges through me. She answers, still sobbing into the receiver. "Claire, I need you to call all the local hospitals. We need to find out if she's been brought to one."

"Ok," she whimpers. "I'll start calling them."

Before I've hung up, I'm already out my door. As

soon as I'm in my car, I speed the entire way to the airport. I arrive, finding the airport in chaos. Police officers are working to corral travelers safely out, others are working with men in suits, some are monitoring the frantic people in the long lines at the check-in desks. I approach the nearest officer. "Sir, can you tell me anything about the flight? My girlfriend was on flight 422."

"I'm sorry, Sir. All I know at this time is that all flights have been temporarily suspended, medical and emergency personnel have responded to the crash scene, and all injured travelers have been taken to the nearest available hospitals."

"Thank you." Stepping away, I reach for my phone and dial Claire. "Did you find her?"

Her sobs weaken my stomach. Nausea forms as my body aches with fear.

"She's not at any of the hospitals. What if she's gone, Grayson? What if she's gone?"

Tears are burning behind my lids. I'm a man who hasn't cried since college, but if I've lost her, there's nothing that will keep this pain from destroying me. Breathing shallow breaths, I lean against the wall. The tall, blond-haired officer I spoke with, steps near.

"Sir, are you all right? Do you need medical attention?"

Leaning forward, resting my hands on my knees, I focus on taking breaths. I've fucking lost her. My Emma—the most incredible woman to ever come into my life. From the moment I first kissed her, I knew I needed more, so much more. Her wit, quirky humor, and appreciation for all things romantic stole my heart before I ever felt what it was like to be inside her. There was never going to be any other woman for me. She was the one person to see me for the damaged man I am and still love me. She was it. It was always her.

"Sir? Are you all right?"

My voice catches and it's difficult to speak, while fighting back the damn tears. "I did this to her. I'm the reason she got on that flight, why she took that job, and now she's gone." The pain is unbearable, consuming me. I fight for more breaths.

"I'm sorry for your loss. Do you have someone that can take you home?"

"Grayson!" Her voice cuts through the chaos of the crowds and the noise erupting from every direction.

Adrenaline pumps through me as I raise my head, searching for her. "I heard her! Where is she? Help me look. She has long, dark hair and is wearing black pants and a red blouse."

"Grayson!"

The officer and I turn our heads the same direction. He points right at her. "There! Is that her?"

"Yes, that's Emma!" Relief slams into me like an ocean tidal wave. Breaking through the crowd, she runs to me. The moment she's in my arms, I hold her close, kissing her hair, and rubbing her back. To have her here, now, with me, it's a feeling I can never describe. All I know is her presence makes the broken parts of me whole again.

Cupping her face in my hands, I kiss her long and deeply. "How are you here in front of me?" I stare into her beautiful eyes, wiping away the tears rolling down her cheeks.

"I didn't get on my flight. I chose you, Grayson. I chose you."

EPILOGUE

GRAYSON

ne Year Later...

MEGAN AND I PLANNED IT all. It's Emma's 30th birthday and we invited all her friends and family to Emma's and my condo for the big, birthday bash. Megan texted that she'll be arriving with her at any moment. This party isn't starting with a joined shout of *Surprise*! though. I've planned a little something special for her arrival. The furry, black and tan Yorkie squirms in my arm, eager to be let free. Adjusting his collar, I ensure the engagement ring is still snugly attached.

The door opens, both women laughing as they enter. The sound of Emma's voice immediately brings me joy. Hidden in the dark, I set the puppy down, letting it run to their feet. He does just as I hoped and

Emma squeals when she sees him. "Oh my God! He's adorable!"

She lifts him up and I cue Claire to hit the lights. Emma's eyes brighten with joyful tears as she looks directly at me. Her hand is on the collar, her fingers have found the ring. I approach, meeting her beautiful gaze and lower to one knee. "Will you do me the honor of being my wife?"

"Yes!" she says between tears. "Yes, Grayson. I love you!"

Standing, I take her into my arms. "I love you too, Princess. More than anything in this world."

SITTING IN MY LEATHER CHAIR, a scotch in hand, I watch Emma sleeping soundly in our bed, a tiny, little dog snuggled next to her. It was one year ago today that I thought I'd lost her. It was her faith in us that saved both our lives. She chose not to take the job in Atlanta, to be with me instead. I found her after she'd been held up at the airport, filling out paperwork at the luggage claim department to ensure her luggage was returned. A flock of birds had damaged the plane's turbine engines, causing the crash, and chaos to erupt. She was further detained by law enforcements' efforts to contain the chaos, and unable to reach me via phone.

By luck or by miracle, that day ended with her in my arms and in my bed. I've never let her out of either a single day since. She's my everything. The one woman to break through my barriers and show me how amazing, crazy and incredible loving her can be.

Setting the glass on the bookstand, I move to our bed. Carefully, I lift the little dog and place him in his bed on the floor. He whimpers and Emma stirs. "Grayson?"

"Right here."

Raising the blanket, I crawl under, joining her. She moves into my arms and I take hold of her hips, sliding her on top of me. She straddles me, giving tender and sensual kisses. "I love you, Grayson Cole."

Lifting my hand to her face, I stroke her cheek. She leans her head into my touch. "I love you, Emma, with every breath I take."

Against my lips, she whispers. "Make love to me."

She rocks over my growing erection. I turn her onto her back and she reaches down and strokes me. "My dirty little, Princess, always so needy for me."

She grins, then giggles as I nip at her neck. "Always."

Thank you for reading My Hot Boss! I hope you enjoyed meeting Grayson, the panty-melter, and the woman with enough sass and spirit to capture his heart! If you you're ready for another panty-melter alpha and sassy heroine romance, then begin book 1 in my Kings MC Romances, with Castle of Kings!

CASTLE OF KINGS
Jake Castle

When he walks into a room, he owns it. From the moment he set eyes on me, he decided I was his. No one - not even my brother, Nix - was going to tell him otherwise. It doesn't matter that Nix is President of the Kings' MC Club. Jake wants what he wants, and he'll set out to get it, whatever the cost.

Jake may be an arrogant asshole, but there's no denying the hold he has over me. His fierce, carnal need to make me his, and his alone, is a snare I can't escape. And truth be told, I don't want to.

But when my life becomes threatened, Jake Castle is the only man my brother trusts to protect me. He knows Jake will do anything to keep me safe.

Anything.

"Jake Effing Castle. The man drips sin and seduction and makes every woman melt with his panty dropping good looks and deep erotic voice. His tatted and hard muscled body has earned his playboy rep but he's about to meet his match.

Betty Shreffler has created quite a world with the Kings MC. It's dark and gritty in some spots, fully realistic, rough and tough, and full of sensual heat. The writing is flawless and descriptive while the sex scenes will set your Kindle on fire. SMOKIN' hot and that's all thanks to my new book boyfriend - Jake Castle. There's action and an excellent plot that unfolds among some excellent word building. My perfect 5 star read!" ~
Picky Bitches Book Blog

Find Castle of Kings at bettyshreffler@yahoo.com!

Join my newsletter for new releases, book discounts, and book news - Subscribe at bettyshreffler@yahoo.com!

Turn the page for a Chapter 1 preview of Castle Of Kings...

CHAPTER 1

CASTLE OF KINGS

Liz

*A*s I approached the aged, wood sided Kings' MC house, it felt as if the last four years hadn't changed a thing. Harleys lined the side of the street due to the overflowing parking lot. The sound of music and voices carried well beyond the walls, sending a sensation of nostalgia straight through me.

I glanced up at my brother, Nix, and took in his appearance. Four years had given him a few extra creases around his vibrant green eyes, but he's still as good-looking and fit as the last time I saw him. While I was away at nursing school, he kept up the bike shop and bar, helping to pay my tuition. If not for him, I wouldn't have been able to return home with my Bachelor's in Nursing.

Being completely out of touch with the current club members had my stomach fighting a slow swirl of nervous butterflies. My feet began to lag on my way up the steps.

"Why the hell did I agree to come here?"

Nix rested his hand on my shoulder and ushered me toward the entrance, a grin splitting his lips.

"It'll be fun," he assured me.

"You know I don't do your parties."

"Trust me, you'll have a good time. My brothers will be on their best behavior with you here. Besides, there's a couple of them I'd like you to meet. I could see you hitting it off."

"I must have been desperate to agree to this."

"Liz, you always think my brothers are wild misfits," Nix chuckled. "Well they are, but that's not all we are. There's so much more to the club and the men who belong to it."

"You mean beers, bikes, and women?" I snickered, turning to face him.

Nix's face twisted into a frown. "How about the charity rides and events?"

I let out a breath in self-resignation. "Fair enough. And what is the event tonight?"

"A charity auction *and* it's fight night."

"Fight night?"

"Yeah, you'll see later. The guys will place bids and whoever wins gets his choice of whatever he wants. Most take cash, some pick something out of the shop for their bikes, some have special requests. Whatever they want. That's the rules."

"This should be interesting."

As we reached the doors, a cacophony of voices, clinking glasses, and boots shuffling the floor mixed with the loud, heart-pumping music in the background. Nix pushed the doors open and placed his hand on my lower back, guiding me into the crowd. Familiar faces, wearing the usual black vests or jackets with the silver skull and crown, lifted from their conversations and waved at us.

Nix stopped at the first table and began his evening of playing host. Being naturally social and a man feared as much as he is revered, he fits the role perfectly. When our Uncle Dallas who'd practically raised us passed away, he left the bike shop and bar to Nix. Nix couldn't have been happier to take over. Nix was a spitting image of Dallas in every way—looks and personality. The discussion of whether or not Nix really was Dallas' kid had come up in conversation a few times among the club members, but that rumor was never proven. Our mother took off on us when we were kids, and we haven't seen her since. Our father died from cancer a couple years later, leaving his brother, Dallas, the responsibility of raising two rebellious pre-teens. To everyone's surprise, we turned out to be well-behaved human beings, most of the time.

"You look beautiful tonight," my Aunt May crooned in my ear. Meeting her gaze, I took in the longer length of her hair and the new gray streaks accenting her amber eyes. She twisted one of my long, loose, dark curls around her finger and flipped it off my shoulder. "Nix will have to keep a protective eye on you. Every man in here is going to want your attention."

"Well, Aunt May," I clicked my tongue against my cheek, "you know my attention is hard to get."

"That's my girl. Make those men work for that tail." With one swift slap, her hand came across my ass.

"You're too much." Shaking my head, I grinned at my spirited Aunt. I pointed toward the bar, getting Nix's attention. "I'm getting a drink."

He nodded and continued on with his meet and greets. Aunt May walked with me to the wood top bar, the Kings emblem mounted proudly on the wall behind it. I rested on the stool and smiled at the long-time bartender, Jeff.

"Two shots of blackberry bird dog and a beer to chase it down."

"On the house, Liz." He set the drinks on the counter and slid them toward us. "Nice to see you. It's been a while."

"Thanks, Jeff. It's good to see everyone."

Aunt May tapped my leg and raised her shot glass, waiting for me to take mine. I lifted it and clinked hers before tilting the glass to my lips.

"We missed you around here." Jeff set his elbows on the bar and leaned forward. "It's good to have your shining face back."

"She was too smart to stick around." Aunt May

pushed her empty glass toward Jeff. "Went off and got herself an education. I'm proud of you, doll."

"Thanks May. I enjoyed nursing school, but I'm glad to be back home. It's not the same anywhere else."

"Of course not." Jeff picked up the empty shot glass and it disappeared under the counter. "This is where your family is. This is your home."

Lifting the beer from the counter, I swiveled my stool and looked over the crowd of club members and those who accompanied them.

"Yes, it is."

I'd grown up in this environment. A place where everyone looked out for each other and treated one another as family even if you weren't blood. I knew just about everyone in the room, save a few new members who'd joined while I was away. These people were my family and it was good to be home.

Across from the bar, a man walked in wearing a black, leather jacket with the familiar club patches and a worn-out ball cap. I couldn't see his face, but I noticed the way others reacted to him. Several women adjusted their cleavage before following him like lovesick puppy dogs. A group of guys by the pool table nodded their heads, and he moved in their direction, ignoring the women as if they didn't exist. They pouted their ruby red lips and slunk back to their tables.

Pointing my beer in his direction, I asked Aunt May who he was. She looked through the crowd to the man I was watching. He shimmied out of his jacket, and I couldn't stop watching the show. The lights over the pool table highlighted layers-upon-layers of rock hard muscles covered with black ink from wrists to shoulders. His chest stretched out the black tank he wore tucked into his dark, denim, ripped-up jeans and studded belt.

"That's Jake Castle. He joined the Kings shortly after you left."

"What's his story?"

"He's from Georgia, but somehow ended up here in Nashville. He became fast friends with Nix and Trevor. He became a member pretty quickly after that."

"Huh." I glanced at Nix who was still making his rounds. "I should bring Nix a beer. He can't seem to get away from his fans." I turned to Jeff. "Can I have another?" I asked, waving my beer at him.

With a pat to my leg, Aunt May returned my attention to her.

"Nix's done well while you were away. The Club has benefitted from his leadership. The shop and bar are doing good, and he's even built a relationship with local law enforcement. The Kings help keep an eye on things, you know, in places they can't."

"What about the other crew? The Wild Royals still around?"

"Unfortunately, yes. They opened a bar on the other side of town. They've been competition. The word is they're running drugs through the bar."

"Of course, they are. Wouldn't expect anything less of them. Correction, yes, I would."

Jeff brought the other beer, and I left Aunt May to

take it to Nix. He gave me a profound thank you and wrapped his arm around me.

"Liz, I want you to meet Dillon," Nix nodded to a handsome guy with messy blond hair, blue eyes, and a large red and black tribal tattoo spiraling around his right arm.

"Nix says you just got back from nursing school. Congratulations."

"I did, thank you. It's good to be home."

"Are you staying for good?"

"Yeah, I've put in a few applications at the local hospitals. Hopefully, something will come of it."

"I'm gonna get the auction going. I'll get with you later, Liz."

Leaving me with Dillon made it clear he was one of the guys Nix hoped I'd *hit it off with*. So far, Nix wasn't wrong. Dillon was attractive with a deep voice and sexy Australian accent.

"Want another one before it gets crazy in here?" Dillon pointed to my nearly empty beer.

"Sure, thank you." I walked with Dillon to the bar and took the same stool as before while Dillon ordered us another couple of beers.

"Nix says you like to go riding."

"I do, yeah."

"Wanna go with me sometime?"

"I might," I cocked my head and grinned.

Dillon chuckled. "Nix warned me you wouldn't be easy to win over."

"Maybe you can coax me with dinner and a ride," I smiled behind my new bottle of beer.

"I'm definitely up for that. What do ya like to eat?"

"Italian."

"I know a place. How about tomorrow at seven?"

"You don't waste time, do ya, Aussie?"

"Not in a place like this, you don't," Dillon winked at me and gave a cheeky grin, "and not when a woman is as attractive as you are. There's gonna be guys lining up to ask you out."

"So far, you're at the front of this non-existent line."

Dillon's smile turned to a frown. I followed his eyes and turned my stool to see who he was looking at. The man with the ball cap and black tank top was standing next to me ordering a beer. He glanced at me and winked, then flashed a pearly white smile with dimples below dark, brown eyes on a face that would melt any woman's panties. I couldn't peel my eyes away from the ripped, tatted, towering hunk of muscle who was making me wet just looking at him.

"You Nix's sister?" He took his beer and leaned against the counter.

"Yeah, Liz."

"He didn't tell me you were gorgeous."

"Well, he didn't tell me anything about you, *at all*. Must have slipped his mind."

Jake let out a chuckle, and I watched his full, kissable lips pull back into a smile. Even his laugh was attractive.

"You gonna be here a while?"

"Probably all night."

"Good. I'll catch ya later, Peach."

"Peach?" I said to Jake's back as he walked away. He looked over his shoulder and winked at me, giving me that same ridiculously charming smile which sparked sexual yearning smack dab between my thighs.

Dillon touched my arm, and I looked over at him, feeling embarrassed I'd forgotten his existence.

"So, is tomorrow at seven good?"

"Oh, yes. Yeah, seven is good. You can pick me up here."

I smiled when I saw Nix approaching the bar. He put his arm around me and pulled me away from Dillon.

"I'll bring her back. I just need her a moment."

Nix guided me to the farthest corner of the room, away from listening ears and the music.

"What's up?" I asked, meeting his serious gaze.

"I see you met Jake."

"Yeah. Is he one of the others you thought I'd hit it off with?"

"No," Nix said coldly. "He's one of the ones I want you to stay away from. Jake's an asshole and a womanizer. I don't want you anywhere near him. Anyone, but him."

Hearing him say that with such passion, brought disappointment burrowing into my chest.

"All right. I'll steer clear of him. Dillon asked me out tomorrow night. Is that okay?"

Nix ran his hand through his lengthy, jet, black hair and let out a breath of relief.

"Yeah, Dillon is a nice guy, but still, don't let him try to take you home."

"Got it, Chief. When's the auction starting?"

"Now. Let's get a seat."

Find Castle of Kings at bettyshreffler.com!

ALSO BY BETTY SHREFFLER

Healed Hearts Romance Collection

FIRE ON THE FARM

MY HOT BOSS

UNBREAK THIS HEART

Kings MC Series

CASTLE OF KINGS

CLIPPED WINGS

KING OF KINGS

Novellas

COUNTDOWN TO CHRISTMAS

View books at: bettyshreffler.com

ABOUT THE AUTHOR

Hi, I'm Betty Shreffler. A USA Today and International Bestselling Romance Author. I writes sexy and suspenseful stories with hot alphas and kickass heroines with twists you don't expect. I also write beautiful and sexy romances with tough women and their journeys at finding love. If I'm not writing or doing book events, you can find me creating book cover designs, snuggling with my dogs watching a movie, or enjoying the outdoors on my motorcycle.

Let's keep in touch!

Join my newsletter for new releases, book discounts, and book news - Subscribe at bettyshreffler.com!

Join Betty's Facebook readers' group: Betty's Book Beauties and Bad Boys

f facebook.com/authorbettyshreffler
BB bookbub.com/profile/betty-shreffler